John Malone Dagnall

Daisy Swain, the flower of Shenandoah

A tale of the rebellion

John Malone Dagnall

Daisy Swain, the flower of Shenandoah
A tale of the rebellion

ISBN/EAN: 9783337137830

Printed in Europe, USA, Canada, Australia, Japan

Cover: Foto ©Andreas Hilbeck / pixelio.de

More available books at **www.hansebooks.com**

THE

FLOWER OF SHENANDOAH.

A TALE OF THE REBELLION.

BY

JOHN M. DAGNALL.

ILLUSTRATED.

BROOKLYN, N. Y.

1865.

CONTENTS.

CHAPTER VI.

CHAPTER VII.

CHAPTER VIII.

CHAPTER IX.

CHAPTER X.

CHAPTER I.

Reuben Swain—His Character—The Birth of Daisy.

LONG ere ruthless civil war laid waste
The fertile Shenandoah Valley, there dwelt,
In all his rustic nature true, and free
As the wind, contented Reuben Swain.   On
A green mound, close by a stream, zigzagging
Like an eel on sandy bed around the vale,
Reuben's lovely home, a neat white cot, stood
Raised on cedar spiles.   This marked his prudent
   mind ;
As ague poisons lurk in meadow damp
And spring freshets had inundate the plain.

No cupola his cottage roof adorned,
Nor did paintings decorate its inner walls
All such ornate pride he left to autocrats,
To tilted lords, and traffic's purse-proud kings.
For, truly, Reuben's nature was too simple
And full of the most gentle virtues as
To even think of such vain, showy things ;
No, his pride was only that of self-respect.
Being one of God's true creatures, Reuben,
Ere each morning sun arose, would upon
His bended knees, at matin prayer, offer
Up his humble thanks to the Giver of all good
For blessings which he hourly conferred,
Of health and vigor, with their many joys,
Cheering his path through life to ripe old age.

Accustomed from his earliest youth to waken
With the day, Reuben always felt a joy
To see, peering through the gray light of dawn,
Streaks of the rising sun, and watch the flush
Of golden light resplendent spread along

The sky ; the verdant landscape o'er illume ;

Tip with purpling gleams the forest pines ;

Disperse the blue mists from the mountain's side.

Then, thus early in the fresh morning air,

Reuben, with supple step, would saunter through

His well-cultured fields ; and, as he trod the grass

Bespangled o'er with crystal dew, he'd watch

With gladsome eye his flocks upon the hillside

Browse, and judge, with reason clear, the yielding

Promise of his crops ; humming to himself,

As with joyous heart he homeward bent his steps,

Some tender breathing of his soul in song ;

For happy as his days were pure, untouched

By gnawing want, unstained by misery,

Lived gentle Reuben in his rural home.

Free he was from fear of loss, from cares, distrust,

The worldly-minded and penurious have ;

From pangs of dire adversity

Attending trade and constant trafficking ;

For in the bounteous vale where Reuben lived,
The only clouds which lower'd were filled with
    rain ;
Reviving parch'd lawn, drooping plant and flower.

Nor could the jade of fickle fortune coquet
With his pride, as vain were all her blandishments
Him to seduce from tranquil state. Yet,
Notwithstanding Reuben's days were balmy
As an Indian summer's cheering glow, still,
His life by no means was a listless dream
Of indolence, of apathy, of sloth ;
For an innate energy to labor
On his acres broad strung his nerves with strength ;
Gave tension to his muscles, suppleness
To his joints, an appetite for food, though
Simple, yet wholesome ; brought sleep to his eyes,
Ease to his mind, and to his heart tranquillity.
Beside, he earned from his patch of land, funds
Enough to keep himself in time of need ;
In case his strength might cease from old age,

Or stricken be by some infirmity.

This was the only selfishness he knew ;

And he took good care the surplus cash which he

Thus saved should cater to no banker's greed,

Nor usury's bait allure it from his grasp,

Nor paper bonds with golden promises ;

For Reuben, in his lifetime, heard much of

Failures, bankruptcy, and breach of trust ;

How in a moment's time the rich, as well

As the poor man's all, had been from them
   swept.

No, Reuben was sole guardian of his gold.

But his hoarded pile filled no chink in a wall,

Nor hole in the ground, but in an oaken chest,

It snugly laid concealed from prying eyes ;

Unsafe, one would think, from prowling burglar,

Whose greed for others' goods, on some dark
   night,

Might tempt his predatory steps to roam

Those parts in quest of spoil, and noiselessly

Sack good Reuben's coffer of its treasure.

But the numbing hand of time had scarcely

Affected Reuben's senses ; for his ear

Was then as quick to catch faint sounds, as when

A boy, hunting squirrels in the wild woods ; .

And therefore sounds of friendly footsteps knew

From the stealthy tread of a sneaking foe.

Nor was his the sluggard's leaden sleep, who

Will, even when his eyes are open, lie

In supine lethargy dozing, peering

Through a misty veil of film ; and blinking

In the light of day, soon again drop off

Unconsciously to sleep.   But no such languor

Blurred the light of Reuben's eyes : once their lids

Were raised, their lamps would brightly burn

   renewed

With vigor's oil, by which he'd soon discern

Strange visions, should they near him flit at night;

Which as soon as seen about, his hand

Would on his gun, already primed to kill

The prowling wolf and panther sly, that sometimes

From their lairs in forests wild came, and raised

Nocturnal havoc 'mong his sheep, be clasped.

Then, as to his neighbors of the plain, Reuben

Knew their habits, tastes, and pedigrees too well

To fear his gold would jaundice their eyes.   They

Reuben's gentle, upright nature also knew ;

Knew that the beam of divine justice shone

In his heart to every one alike within

The valley ; and blending theirs with his, lived

In peace and harmony together :

For each one's sense of equity was just.

Honor was kind Reuben's guide ; probity

Their counsellor ; nothing foul corrupted

Reuben's mind ; nor was his taste depraved ;

His bev'rage was the same that Adam drank :

Water pure from clear springs and rocky founts.

This he knew would poison nought within, nor

Thrill his nerves awhile with spurious ecstacy,

To deaden the keen sensibility

Of body, heart, and soul, like alcohol,

The demon, that fires with delirium

The drunkard's brain, and fills the minds of men

2

With dark designs and treason's treach'rous guilt,
Angry quarrels, murder ; then remorse which
Struggles hard with sleep. No, Reuben would
 shrink
With loathing from the devil's nectared bane,
And aught which tended to engender heat
Of blood, burning thirst, and gusts of passions
 vile.
Temperate wishes only were in his soul.

 The fleecy fabric shorn from his own sheep,
Woven on his own loom, sufficed to guard
His body 'gainst inclement gales, and warm
Him in the fiercest wintry blow ; and in
This simple raiment clad, Reuben felt
As great as any Eastern nabob proud,
Bedecked with royal robes ; as nature's lord
Was he, and reigned supreme in his neat cot,
His castle proud on nature's realms built,
On a green lawn, within a bounteous plain,
Where creation was prolific with her products.

To Reuben 'twas the loveliest spot on earth,

Where many sunny years of bliss he passed,

Sharing the joys of dear domestic life

With the partner of his soul, his Nancy dear,

More faithful, fair, and kind than half of those

Who blaze in vain, proud, ostentatious show :

One who knew her duties well, her womanly

    sphere,

And the sweet pleasures of the virtuous heart ;

Which was the only bliss her husband sought.

There, in the quiet place wherein the happy pair

Found shelter, food, and rest, reason ruled

Their minds and guided them with judgment ; for

Too well they understood the sacred bond,

By which their two dear souls were bound as one,

To mar their wedded bliss with household jars,

Knowing angry breath in ears young is baneful :

And in sweet connubial union their love

Long ago had multiplied itself.   The seed

From vigorous stem was cull'd, and free from

Withering blight ; kind nature undertook

The task imposed ; and time brought forth a bud

Of grace, all tenderness, which doubly blest

Their yoke, and crowned with joy their nuptial

    couch.

The germ in beauty's mould was cast, budded
Forth, and blossomed ; in sacred soil grew up
To vernal morn of life, fresh as a rose
In unmolested shade, or violet chaste
In all its virgin freshness, unassuming,
Modest, all rural grace, and simple charms.

The joy of her pure heart, all smiles, all cheer,
Like rising sunlight on a dewy lawn, shone
On her dimpling cheeks ; rouged with tincture from
Vermeil meads : health's purpling flood that
    coursed in
Her azure veins.

                    The vital essence glowed
In her eyes, radiant, pure, and mild, like two
Bright orbs fixed in the coronet of Heaven :
Endowed they seemed with photographic power
To print from blooming flowers certain shades ;
As they one noon-time bright, while ardently
Fixed upon a variegated bed, drew

2*

By some charmed affinity in their gaze,

Blended hues from both blue-bell and lily ;

And so bright withal, that e'en a lover's glance

    might

Dim before their lustrous beaming, or be

Dazzled so his mind's eye would flashing see

Across his brain, a thousand stars glitt'ring

Resplendent with heavenly jewelry.

  Enrobed in raiment woven plain upon

Her mother's loom, she, by broach or bracelet

Unadorned, looked with more attractive grace

Than if bedecked in fashion's gaudy finery.

Besides, her form was faultless as the Venus

Of Milo, as fair, as tender to the view ;

Required no false blandishments to lure

The eye, nor stuffs to give herself proportion :

Her heart was void of all such guile, as truth,

Early to her God, had risen up her soul

To heaven, where her faith in Him reposed.

Thus arrayed in nature's simple beauty,

Daisy Swain, the flower of Shenandoah,

Since taken from her parent bed, was

Mildly nurtured with parental sway,

And prospered in her father's fostering hands,

Full sixteen years unconscious of a thorn ;

Unstained by care and sorrow's withering sigh :

Nor had she felt the pangs of fickle love,

That sighs assent, then vanishes from sight.

She was her parents' joy ; their dear pledge of

Reciprocal love ; their pride of heart, whom

They idolized with fond, indulgent care.

Truly, Reuben blest his happy lot, as

His dear wife and child made his cherished home

An envied Paradise, remote from power,

Despots, and proud high-toned authority.

For thus in quiet state he lived in vale of peace,

Where nature gave refreshing showers to

Ev'ry living creature in the valley ;

High and low of birth ; and of mean degree.

There, playful zephyr breathed around his cot ;

And feather'd minstrels trilled their dulcet pipes

Melodiously from boughs of hick'ry green

And chestnut, whose leafy branches intertwined

Above its roof, and formed a canopy

Which screened, from scorching mid-day heat, one of

The most happy men on this revolving orb ;

One in whose heart the pure flame of devotion

Burned, whose eye, when raised toward the Great

    Supreme,

Saw His blessed spirit in the heavens

Poised on beams of holy light eternal ;

For in Him who gilds the clouds with serene light,

And moves them at His will, was the faith of

Reuben, who, although with eyes untutored,

Saw the book of God was always open

To His creatures ; bound with blue sky and

    illumed

With mingling tints of hills, woods, and plains,

    which

Marked the pictured landscape as the blessed work

Of Hands unerringly Divine, and governed

By a Mind most potent to control *all*

Within the universal world, His who keeps

An eye benignant on His creatures.

Yes, Reuben saw God's kingly spirit throned

Among the hills, the forests, vales, and wilds ;

And heard His awe-inspiring voice thunder
In the torrent's roar, murmur sweetly in
The tingling rill, and whisper in the breeze ;
Felt His friendship in the warm sunlight, gave
Life, and joy, and hope to those who are not
Tied to earth by doubts and worldly things :
Saw God's glad eye peering through the stars by
　　　night,
In concentric glimpses from His throne of
Glory, where, when heaven would untie
His human bands, Reuben knew full well that
His good soul being from its earthy matter broke,
Would gladly mount the void of viewless air,
And mingle with the spirits of the pure
And holy.

CHAPTER II.

The Comet—The Northern Fanatic—The Southern Demagogue—The First Shot at Sumpter—The Battle—The Wounded Federal.

SCARCE had the shock of party strife begun
To vibrate on the nation's heart, than from out

Its dreadful depths a comet flash'd athwart

The lurid sky, and glanced its fiery gleams

Upon star-gazers' eyes.   They shrank amazed,

With wonder and dismay alternate,

In their breathless stare.   Timid hearts fluttered

With affright.   Their fear-fraught minds imagined

That the face of heaven scowling lowered ;

That darker frowns deformed the brow of night,

Just where the shadow marked its orbit's trail,

Foredooming to their terror-stricken hearts,

That soon their sun of day would be eclipsed

Forever in chaotic darkness.   Even

Those not quite so superstitious foreboded

The celestial visitor ominous

Of evil dire unto Columbia's sons :

Some great misfortune to their nation, torn

By faction, on the brink of dissolution,

Would be rent asunder by domestic foes,

Thirsty for spoils, for power, and ambition.

Alas! thus luckless did the omen prove ;

For dark spirits then in secret conclave

Thronged around us almost everywhere,

Scheming to fire our minds with discontent,

Intensify our party pride to frenzy ;

And to barter our blest inheritance

To secret traitors and the fiend war,

Which often plague the world and banish

Men's repose.

   'Twas in those momentous times,

That, with his hoary head absorbed, hung low

Upon his agitated breast, and with

His anxious visage haggard made by thoughts

Rebellious, there sat alone in his abode

A vulture-beak'd victim of unsated pride, _

Deeply hatching in his subtle brains schemes

The most seditious to disturb the peace

And sever the bond of social life and

Friendship's holy wreaths, which bound us North

  and South.

Matured, some wily thought his bent brows raised.

Quick as a meteor's flash in night's dark sky,

A sudden flush of inward joy lit up

His scowling features.   Then starting to his feet,

He paced, with nervous tread, the tapestry,

And rubbed his hands exultingly at some

Hellish plot his crafty mind conceived.

'Twas to kindle with incensive breath,

The igneous volcano of rebellion,

Smouldering in the breasts of freemen South :

For, the aim of all his life had been to earn

In their mad struggles, the short-lived glories

Of a puffed-up name, e'en tho' 'twere coupled

With foul and blasting infamy, likewise

His country's disgrace.   'Twas this false honor

Alone inspired his dark soul and made him,—

Hoping to attain his wished-for height—

Venal both to his constituents, and

Blushless at his own plans to embroil the States

In brutal, internecine conflict : for,

The fanatic's wily mind did well discern,

In the proud South, the darker shade of

Slav'ry, which to distort from features real was

The sole purpose of his crafty fancy.

There, upon his mental vision glittered,

From the Ethiopian's brow, a diamond black :

The dazzling prize so touched his covetous soul,

That down he knelt before his black idol ;

Crouched, spaniel-like, to kiss its feet ;

Turned up the white of his eyes to'ards heaven,

And implored the Lord on high to befriend

The poor, fat, dusky son of Africa,

Manacled with chains, which made his pierced
    heart .

Wail echoes the year round to their clanging sounds.

What sanctified disguise, base hypocrite!

What a feint delusive the hand of power

To grasp! Was it not a mask most guileful

Through which you sought to gain your own bad
    ends?

For you could well dissemble and disguise

Your dangerous intents.

                      Thus, under pretence

Of human good and his country's honor,

The favorite side he joined, the people's votes

By subtle craft and subterfuge to win:

In stately halls shrieked freedom for the blacks,

To a gloomy, narrow-minded concourse

Of visionary bigots and fanatics:

Told how the slaves in servile chains lingered

Out a life far worse than death itself; and how

Their cruel masters flayed them so, till, through

Their lacerated flesh, their bones protruded.

"We must rise," he said, "and overwhelm

In one common ruin, these brute men ; must wrest

The beastly chattels from the monsters ; and if

Opposed by them in our incursions on

Their soil, our heels, where'er they tread, ruins

Ruthless marks must print whilst liberating

From their cruel bonds, a disfranchised, abused,

Unpitied race."

        Such were the views he vented

To his list'ning hosts, whose hearts he fired with

Indignation keen against the slaveholder.

Then him they sanctioned as their party choice ;

Rose him with their fulsome breath and votes from

Common life to an exalted station :

For, on the tide of popular favor,

Soon he floated into office, to rule

And glitter like a meteor for an hour.

    *   *   *   *   *   *   *   *   *

Meantime, in the haughty South, a demagogue

Urged, from the rostrum, in the slave mart,

Excited, discontented freemen,

To spurn all future refuge 'neath the "flag

Whose starry folds wrapt freedom in her grave."

His ambition burned in ruthless deeds ;

For his pride was that of glaring pomp, love

Of conquest, and of fame that might resound

Through vaulted skies, till times remote should

    hand

His glories down in the historic page.

There, the weak•mortal to true glory blind,

Stood venting forth the fervid emanations

Of his own proud, domineering soul, in

Gestures like the antics of an idiot,

To a crowd of lawless bullies, youths, and men,

Inciting them to raise the standard of

Revolt against their lawful government.

He said : the crisis called them to their duty ;

That if they would be freemen, they must leave

Their peaceful homes for high aims to attain,

By taking arms up in defense of State rights ;

That their firesides and altars were endangered

By a factious horde of galling bigots,

Then installed in office, who would them govern

With an iron rod, just as their ruthless wills

Proposed : invade their sacred fields, ransack

Their homes, and free, without law or price, their

    slaves.

Thus harangued the fire-eating scorpion

With wrathful tongue unruly, soon he fired

His listeners' minds and hearts with loud

    complaints

Of tyranny. Tyranny ! in a land

Where independence lifts her dauntless brow,

And where freedom is Columbia's boast !

" If we had withered in the womb," he cried,

" Or that when we were infants at the breast,

Our mothers had, with deadly nightshade smear'd

Their nipples o'er, and then had, with their milk

Thus impregnated with the bane of death,

Suckled us to graves untimely, better

It would have been, than for us now to smother

In our freeborn hearts the chiding curse

Of Northern foes, whose galling enmity

Has, in the South, Liberty's bright sun dimm'd

With Discord's blackest cloud.

                     "But, friends, I say,

Let the infernal band of livid spectres

Of despair once cross our path ; the horde of

Hell-born snakes will in their warpèd skins

Shrink dismayed before our might and strength :

We'll our bright meads redden with their blood ;
     heap

With their marrowless bones, the pageant death,

On ev'ry Southern plain ; while, with shot, with

Shell, and murd'ring knife, we shall their States
     invade :

Ay, plant as many bayonets on their fields

As there are blades of grass.   Therefore, valiant

Be.   Endure with fortitude the toils of

War.   Be warriors all in conflict, nor let

One of you a coward turn ; but when you find

The dastard Yankee wounded, bleeding out

His craven spirit on the ground, permit

No soft, mawkish pity your tears to crave,

As the hardest heart will sometimes melt 'fore

Dying eyes, but let your own eyes at him roll

With fiery scorn.   Let all your breath be charged

With Anger's poison ; and like a serpent

Hiss into his ears the venom'd bane ; you damn'd,

Sneaking, lily-livered Yankee, die ;

We no quarter show, no mercy have

For nigger-thieves ; then with your bayonets pin

Him to the ground."

            Then, loud his maddened hosts,

With wild hurras, the demagogue applauded ;

Swore that they'd with fire and sword do deeds of

Ruthless stamp ; would pillage, burn, leave behind

Them death in every Yankee town ; and bear

Ensanguined trophies to their free-made homes ;
Map out through fell havoc on rebellious soil,
A nation of their own, for them to fix,
Till doomsday came, a firmer yoke upon
Their slaves.

    *   *   *   *   *   *   *   *   *

Then soon the startling news on wings of lightning
Flashed through ev'ry part of fair Columbia's land ;
That, in the South, insurgents were, with bombs,
Shelling freedom's starry ensign on
Sumter's isolated fort, waving.
Retribution, thereupon, was promised
By the North.   Futile were all peace petitions
To avert the strife ; as rage vindictive
Was too blind for moral arbitration ;
And yet both sides were base enough to call
Upon high Heaven, in the clash to aid them.

    Sounds of trumpet, drum, and shrilling fife were
Heard through all the land, rousing men to arms,

Hurrying on the deadly conflict by

Parasites and cowards, both of North and South,

Who feared to stain their own right hands in

Human gore ; and from window, pole, and peak,

Waved the civic garland of our liberties,

Inspiring chivalrous men to furious fight.

Then songs and bloody hymns were sung by sons

Undaunted, as they thro' the madden'd nation

March'd straight on to the red fields of slaughter,
    there

With dearest blood to fertilize the soil,

And earn, in righteous cause, a glorious name.

Soon war and rapine wild, both far and near,'stalked

Madly o'er Virginia's soil.   There, down in

The fertile valley of the Shenandoah,
Resounded loud red War's fierce rattle.   There
Advancing hosts of bannered foemen met,
Emblazoned gay, in pride of fancy dress,
And charged each foremost line with musketry.
Alert, the rebels bold with desperate dash
Hurled, with all their ardor wild, their forces strong
Upon their Federal foes.   Fiercely flashed
The red artillery.   Swiftly shrieking shells

Burst in among the brave, and made their blood

In torrents flow.   Then bayonets charged and

   clashed

Against each glitt'ring blade.   Horse and rider

Plunged into the fray, and swelled the mortal strife

Of battle hot : while Death, through sulph'rous

   clouds

Of smoke, grinn'd and gloated as he eyed firm

Heroes, from their shattered lines and columns,

Fall and swell the slaughter ; and where the

   maimed

Lay, here and there, upon the gory field,

Rending the air with fitful cries and groans,

Writhing, like wounded snakes, from horrid

   tortures.

   So, in full retreat and loose array, down

The hill the Federals wildly rushed, o'erwhelm'd ;

Rank and file, hard pressed by the rebels :

Through thickets dense, 'cross fertile fields and

   vales,

Dismayed their broken columns flew, leaving

On that bloody field many comrades brave,

Who now sleep in their trench-dug sepulchres.

Yet, one among the federal bands, wounded

And faint from loss of blood, footsore, halted

At a gurgling brook, where he, all smeared with

His life-blood, stooped down ; and, in the hollow

Of his right hand, scoop'd drops of water few,

With which his burning thirst he quenched.

                   Then, from

The margin of the stream, he tried to raise himself,

Fearing, lest he there too tardy stayed, captured

He might be by some disloyal enemy

Prowling rampant round those parts, in hot
    pursuit

Of straggling and of ambushed foes : but irksome

Was the task.   The sinews of his knees

Were void of strength. His tired limbs the burden

Of his body could not bear.   A shudder

Shook his jaded frame : 'twas the harbinger

Of comfortless despair which soon darkened

His fevered brain ; for, ere long, his head grew

So giddy, that the verdant landscape seemed

Unto his blurred eyes, just like a green mist

Risen from the ground.   Then, round and round,
     his head

Reeled.   Faint and sick at heart, he stagg'ring
     grasped,

With feeble hands, a willow twig dangling

Near him ; and with its friendly aid lower'd

Himself down upon the damp grass, resolved

To abide the ordeal of strengthless fate.

   Then wrapping himself up in the standard

Which he through a hard campaign had borne :
     happy

In the thought that should his eyes ne'er open
     more

To view the morning's light, its starry folds

Would be, at least, his shroud obsequious.

So, weary, worn, all gnashed, exhausted, quite

Resigned, he let his weak frame throb and
    struggle
'Gainst his parting life upon the humid ground,
Where outstretched full length he lay beneath
A spreading willow, whose pliant branches
Waved above, and soothingly fanned his face,
All gaunt and spectre-like : yet, though grim
His features were, and shaded with the hue of
Death, still, in their fine outlines remained
Traces symmetrical, showing that they had
Been in the fairest mould of beauty cast.

But his fevered mind soon somnolent became.
In dreamy mood he thought of the home he'd left
Behind him, and of his aged mother
Far away : he fancied he saw her smile ;
And with her arms outstretched in fullness of
Joy, ready to clasp to her fond bosom
Her soldier son. He, likewise, thought he heard
Her soft voice say, "Oh ! Athol dear, how glad
Am I to see that you have home returned
4*

From the rebellious, frantic scheme, with none

But honored scars." Then, thoughtful, he smiled ;
    but

'Twas only a sickly gleam of joy,

As pale and transient as a streak of sunlight

Breaking through a rain-cloud, which shone upon

His wan face : for soon the past joys of home

And friends, his ardent fancy had conjured,

Quickly vanished before his reason's strength,

And left his mind in dark, despondent gloom.

Then he wept ; for he keenly realized

The true condition of his hapless plight

And how fallacious was the hope, in such

A dying state, of ever sharing, with

His tender parent, her gladsome care again.

Ah, then, he knew no good Samaritan

Was nigh with balm to heal his wound ; nor did

He hear an angel's light foot fall upon

The ground, bringing an assauging draught to ease

His racking pains.   No, he gave up his life

As lost, for each moment he heavier breathed,

And louder by spells, he groaned from his aches,

And also thought he heard the voice of death,

In the hollow moaning of the wind,

That fretful sighed around him : a fitful gust

Of which, just then, from off his temples smooth,

Detached some beaded drops of fevered sweat

Which clung like dew upon a lily's leaf

On his pale brow : one pellucid globule

Roll'd upon his half-closed eye-lash ; its gleam

His wand'ring mind, and vision dim, mistook

For the glitter of the vestal star twinkling

Through the willow's foliage above his head.

'Twas then twilight, yet no friendly succor

Came to his aid. Alone, the evening dew,

As 'twere, seemed to commiserate him, in

His hapless state, with tears compassionate

Shed on his languid form ; and when he saw

The light of day fast fading from his view,

Hope's bright beam flickered in his panting heart.

Still, he'd judge it folly to repine 'gainst

What Heaven ordained, as his conscience told
    him

That man, soever good, and soldier brave,

Are sometimes in this checquered life destined

To suffer torturing ills, which often

Bring them, ere their lives have run the length of

The allotted span, down to early graves.

    But it would, he thought, have been more
      honorable

If fate, with her unerring hand, had hurled

Upon the field, rebellion's missile swift

Through his brain ; so that he could have fallen

'Mong many warring hosts unknown, but brave,

And mingled his with their courageous blood,

Than there, with feelings sore, linger and waste

Away by fever ; be flesh-conquered ; die

And rot : his body fill no hallowed vault

Nor soldier's grave, but lie exposed, where

Buzzards sought their prey : he shudder'd at the
　　thought,
And gasping, shrieked aloud, they soon would
Fly around his bier and riot on
His lifeless flesh.

CHAPTER III.

Reuben's Alarm at the Sound of Battle—Daisy's
Absence from the Cot—Her Return Home
with the Wounded Soldier.

UPON the balmy breeze of that same morning '
Reuben, the peasant, from his smiling cot,
Heard the battle's horrid din resound,
And saw, afar, thick, sulphurous smoke dimly
Rear in black wreaths to'ards the glaring sun.
'Twas but an hour before the valley rang
With war's alarm, that in the morning ray, he
O'er his neat fields trod ; nor feared to meet
Friend or enemy of the warring bands.
Both were foes to him.

                    For when the roar of
Booming cannon echoed on his startled ear,

He thought that ere the evening came, he'd look

Upon his burning cot and wander round

A homeless man.   But twilight came.   Long since

The battle's warlike blasts had died away ;

And glad he was to find his fields were still

Adorned with waving grain.

But when he saw

His beloved child was not at home to cheer

Him with her pleasing smile, and bless him at

The   evening   board,   a   poignant   pang   went

    straight

To his heart, that some mishap his daughter

Had befallen.

For no tidings of her had

Arrived, since, in the gleam of morning's sunshine,

Her father's cot she quit, to saunter through

Her native vale ; and blithe and jocund wind

Amid its green retreats ; joyously scent

The woodbine wild, and quaff the balmy air ;

And to let the zephyr of fragrant meads
Mellow in deeper tints her beamy face.

But as she gayly tripp'd with fawn-like steps,
Through green paths, observing with enraptured
    eye,
The varied landscape o'er—her soul's delight—
And breathing sylvan sweets with spirits gay,

War's infernal gong through the surrounding hills,

Reverbrated loud and pierced her ears.

The dread shocks her heart's blood stagnated.
　　Fear

Forced its livid pallor o'er her roseate cheeks,

Which marred awhile the lustre of their bloom.

But the rose ne'er drooped.　The shock was but

A passing gust, which chilled awhile her warm
　　blood,

As she soon revived and glowed again in

All her fullness of sweet budding charms.

　　Then curiosity's incentive power

Entered her timid heart, and allured her

To a hillock's rocky crest hard by, to view,

If possible, the spot contentious where

Warring discord waved his flaming brand ; where

Freemen's hands fraternal were in kindred gore

Being imbrued.　For she, long hidden from

The busy world in her elysian home,

Knew not what misfortune's cloud o'ershadowed

Then her sunny plain and leafy bowers,
Wherein some sixteen joyous springs she'd past,
Unknown to woes and cank'ring tortures keen.

Thence far across the Shenandoah plain,
Looming o'er its richly-cultured fields,
She saw the smoke of battle curling rise
In clouds beneath the sun that fiery glared,
On her astonished sight, through a black'ning pall,
Which rose up from the scene of carnage. Wrapt
In amazement, she wondered at the sounds
The battle storm awoke, and why they roared
Unabated through the peaceful valley.

Ah ! she little dreamt that then the reign of
Peace and order in the North and South had been
Overthrown ; that 'twas the unhallowed work
Of bold, bad men, compelled to relinquish
Their high seats in senate halls ; and others
Who long nursed in hot-beds of human fraud
And folly, had nearly all their life-long lives

Devoted their time and talents to grasp

The nation's spoils and tamper with its laws ;

That Columbia's realms, once free to all

Mankind in language, conscience, creed—domains

Extending from New Hampshire's snow-capped
    cliffs,

As far as California's golden shores,

Wherein blest content, prosperity, and

Holiest liberty all fraternal dwelt,

Were then ruled by usurpation's edicts,

More galling to a people free than any

Arrogant ukase of a tyrant proud,

Who trembles night and day upon his throne.

At length the din of battle paused upon

Her ears.   Twilight shadows round her gathered ;

And setting sun-beams faintly gleamed upon

A rolling cloud, whose ruffled crest, bright plumed

With crimson tints, passed o'er her.   Thus
    forewarned

Of night approaching the shadowy rock,

On which she sat, up she quickly rose, and
Down through the hillside's winding paths she ran
Towards the cot.

        Scarce had she neared a glade,
Ere she heard, upon the evening wind, screams
Of woe.   Bewildered quite, she quickly turned
Around and gazed about, above, below ;
Peeped through the murky glare of eve, but
    nothing
Saw of life. Then she wondered whence the sound
Arose, and what it could have been : listen'd
Like a hare startled by game-dogs on the scent :
Still, all was silent round, save the rustling
Of leaves, the barking of tree-toads, whimp'ring
Of bats, and the incessant buzz of insects,
Holding their nocturnal jubilees.

  So, she fancied that the wail she heard was
Perhaps a catbird's woful mew, and hasten'd
On again along her woodland way.   But ere

Her nimble feet had measured paces few,

The groan again, more agonizing still,

Burst on her ears.   Appalled at the sound, she
   shrank,

Like the tendrils of a fragile flower

In a chill autumnal gust of wind, still.

Soon her doubting fears were gone ; as, she knew

Full well that such a sad lament could only

From a human soul distressed issue.

                              Then, soon,

Compassion moved her.   Through a willow copse

She hied, slow pacing cautiously, and reached

The margin of the stream where lay half dead,

The wounded soldier.   Soon the tender fair one

Tremblingly bent o'er him and closely scann'd

Him with her pity-gleaming eyes.   She saw

The light of life still flickered in his heart ;

But wav'ring on the balance side of death

Whose shadow glimly danced upon his features,

Which in their livid aspect seemed to her

So beautiful, so mild. Then, with mute surprise,
She viewed his anguished mien, and wound all
    bare :
And dropt in cleansing tears, the limpid chlorine
Of her soul, upon his bleeding scar.
A transitory smart he felt. He muttered
"Oh !" and casting up his glassy eyes, he saw,
Low bending o'er him, so grateful in the gloom,
And all compassionate, the maiden fair in
White robe meekly clad.

                    "O Heavenly Father !
What angel from thy throne of glory hath
Fled, to chant the sad requiem o'er my cold clay ?"
He cried. "One whom a ruling Providence
Hath hither sent, the friendless to befriend,
The helpless to save," she cried : saying which,
She brushed the matted locks back from his
    brow.
Then, she from her side a napkin took,
Saturated o'er with dew, and with it laved

His pallid brow ; his parched lips moistened ;
   plucked
A plantain leaf which on the streamlet's margin
Grew, and with its cooling texture improvised
A bandage for his wound ; then tied it with
A ringlet of her auburn hair.

                                     Meanwhile,
She made his prospects of recovery bright ;
Told him, that not far from thence safe, nestled
In a grove, he would within her father's cot
A refuge find. This cheering hope his soul
Elated. Forthwith his glad heart urged his hand
To be extended to the gentle maid.
She took it kindly in her own and raised,
With all the strength her fragile structure had,
Him from the blood-stained ground. Faltering,
He leaned his right arm on her shoulder. Halting
At alternate steps to breathe. Well she bore
The burden of his weight, without a murmur,
With maidenly resolution all the way

Thro' thicket paths, 'cross glades ; guided only
By the light which faintly glimmer'd from the cot.

Then, soon before its wicket gate they stood.
Quick the maiden pushed it open ; as quick
Upon its thongs elastic back it swung,
And grated harshly on the latch.   The pointer
Barked and quickly scented the stranger ; while
The father to his feet started up, grasped
His gun, and to the door ran just as she knocked.
The gentle tap he knew came from his daughter.
Quick the door flew back, creaking on its hinges,
Upon the threshold stood the anxious father,
With extended arms to clasp his daughter ;
But back a pace he bounded, as his eyes
In started sockets stared upon his child,
All fagged, all faint, with the feeble soldier.

Soon the mute appeal of Athol's wound went
To the parents' hearts.   Warm commiseration
Thawed from out their breasts the icy chill of fear,

As they soon placed him on a mattress near

Some hick'ry faggots blazing, a helpless,

But a welcome guest beneath their roof.

                                        O'er

His prostrate form they hung in speechless trance,

And gazed in artless grief upon the gash

A bayonet's point had in his right arm

Punctured.   Quickly, from the orifice of

The ugly scar, the mother cleansed with

Water warm, the fetid pulse that flowed ;

Then, with a linen bandage, moisten'd o'er

With arnica, the wound she neatly bound

Within its styptic folds, and left it so ;

To nature's healing care and time for due
     amendment.

This done, the daughter from her mother's
     hand—

The one nearest her sympathetic heart—

Took a strength'ning draught ; a potent febrifuge

And charmed carminative it was, most

Happily blended, and gave it to him
In doses small, but oft.

                        In due time, it soothed
His fevered brain, allayed his burning thirst,
Stopped his stifled moans of anguish ; and caused
In the accelerated current of
His blood, health, that had in his faint nature
Dormant lain, to mount up to his bloodless cheeks,
And flush them with returning vigor's hue.

Then the bland and soothing influence of
Sleep crept into his wakeful mind ; and deep
From the living world his thoughts immersed in
Her somniferous dews.

                Thus, in soft composure
Wrapt, the parents, as they to their rest retired,
Prayed that Athol's future hardships might bo
Few ; and bade their willing daughter keep
Her midnight vigil near his couch ; raise,
When the fond task required, his wounded arm ;
To prop his drooping head upon the pillow ;
And wait upon her suffering friend as
For a loving brother's pains.

CHAPTER IV.

Athol tells the Cottagers the Story of his Life—
His Convalescence and his Love of Daisy.

At early dawn the wounded Federal,
Much improved in health and quite refreshed in
Spirits from his night's repose, awoke ; and glad
Was he to find himself so near kind friends.
Especially his frail rescuer, who
Then stooped o'er him, with helping hands and
    raised
Him on his pallet soft.   He knew no balsam
For his pains and aches more sanative than
The soothing office in which she was
Engaged, and thanked her for the kind attention
She had rendered.   Daisy curtseyed low and
    said :

That both her mother dear and father had

Taught her, long since, the divine injunction,

" To do good to others forget not ;"

And never, when want and suff'ring implored

Her kind assistance, to withhold relief.

As the impressive tones on Athol's ears

Fell from her lips, his head reclined, entranced

With dreamy thought, which Daisy soon observed :

But she knew not what was passing through his
mind,

Nor why hope's inward beam his count'nance
brighten'd ;

For her gladsome gaze was too intently

Fixed upon his handsome face, admiring

The graceful contour of its features, which,

In his pride of youth, show'd her that scarce had

Twenty summers' blooms their roseate honors
shed

Upon his head.

Then God's voice persuaded

Him to prayer ; and, in a benediction

Which he gave, he prayed that Heav'n kind would
  watch

The generous streams which flowed so purely

In their hearts, from being corrupted by

Misfortune's turgid dregs.

Meantime, all the folks

With Athol's modest mien enraptured felt ;

Yet wondered why a youth so devout of heart

Was in soldier's garb bedeck'd.   But they soon

Dispelled the doubt which then   their minds
  engross'd ;

For they saw, in his ingenuous looks,

Bland and affable deportment, it was

Easy to address him on the subject

Of his life and ventures.   So them he soon

Enlighten'd ; closely they gather'd round him,

And with mute attention drank his accents

As he spoke.

He first, with measured terms,

Denounced the political fomenters of

The North and South : told how they had incited

The rebellion, and brought the country, then, to

    such

A pass with their mad schemes for fame and pelf :

Related, from the day his patriot heart

First burned with martial fire to do battle

For his country, the warlike incidents of

His soldier life : told how high his feelings

Ran, unbiass'd by sect or party, with love

Of duty to the cause of Union, right

Or wrong ; that, being one of the first aroused,

He joined a gallant legion of the North,

One thousand strong, all fine picked men, and

    march'd

Unflinching to the strife, to overpower

The rebel chief's deluded myrmidons ;

To curb the proud, defiant spirit of

The would-be king, who, in his haughty pride,

Wish'd to sit enthroned amid his slaves ; but that

The North had so far baffled his ambition :

That his Confed'racy was but parchment,

Which would, ere long, be all ablaze and scatter'd

To the four winds of earth in charred tinder :

And that the arch-traitor would himself, like

A rabid dog, be driven in a hole

Obscure, and kept there till remorse and grief

Devour'd him, for the murd'rous butcheries

He had caused, the widows and the orphans

He had made.

               Athol, then, recounted o'er

What risks and dangers he had undergone ;

How oft they'd met the foe, and routed him

Through woods, down dales, 'cross floods, and
     over

Ridges blue of Virginia ; till, elated

By so much success, they one day, while

Pushing their course on thro' the Shenandoah,

Were met by the enemy reinforced

With many battalions strong ; and in which

Encounter, for the first time, the hot tide

Of battle turn'd against them ; then described

How they stood the shock of kindred hosts, durin ȝ

Full six hours its seething lava rolled

" Yet," he cried, " altho' the North-men brave fell

Fast and thick around us, still we felt embolden'd

By our other deeds triumphant, that we'd gain

The fight ; but the unequal prowess

Of intrepid Jackson on our right,

Turned the fortunes of the day against us ;

And thousands now of our brave boys lie

Stiff and black upon that bloody field.

Terror-stricken, the remnant of our corps,

Then fled, pell-mell, in all directions ;

And I likewise, wounded as you see, took flight.

But, it seemed that I, alas ! was doomed to meet

A fate worse than that which I had then escaped :

To fall upon the road and die, a prey

To craving hunger, thirst, and loss of blood.

But your noble daughter—God bless her—chanced

To hear my groans ; came where I dying lay ,

And, touched with pity at my hurts, my moans,
And aggravated feverish fits, minister'd,
With her cheering voice, sweet consolation
To me, just as I of hope was nigh bereft.
Then, all gentleness and patient meekness,
Here my guiding angel brought me.

                                    Then as
Athol panting heavily, paused to gain his breath,
The daughter, in the meantime, thought it strange
He'd left his home, his friends and kindred, and
    asked
Him, with tones persuasive, if his mother
Had not bade him stay at home to comfort her
Rather than to risk his life in battle.

  "She did and said : 'Dear Athol, be not rash,
You're too young yet to cope with stalwart men
Inured to camp life, whose trade it is to spill
Their fellow mortals' blood, when passions rife
Contending, bid them strike each other with

Vile implements of death. Why, then, do you,

Athol, so young and innocent, desire to swell

These hordes of harden'd men, perchance

To make your mother a childless parent,

For her with tears maternal to bewail

In agèd widowhood, your dear loss, when   .

Here at home, you've health, rest, and ev'ry com-

fort.' "

Then, the emotions strong in Athol's heart,

Forced, from its clear springs, feeling tears to gush

Into his eyes. A nervous tremor shook

His frame. He back, exhausted, on his pallet fell,

Quite overcome, and wept in his despair,

That p'rhaps, he'd ne'er again, upon this earth, see

His fond parent more.

Touched at such a sight,

Tears warm and sympathetic glistened in

The old folks' eyes. His grief their daughter's

bosom

6*

With compassion moved.   Soon at his side,

His tender friend to pain stooped near him ; and,

With her sweet condoling breath, she whispered

In his ear, the sovereign balm of hope, to heal

His lacerated heart.   He heard her voice, looked

Up, and saw the cherub bending o'er him.

Soon the cheering soul-light of her eyes absorb'd

The grieving streams which coursed his anguish'd

    cheeks,

And lighten'd up his abject mind. From the
Earliest to the latest hour the dear fond girl
Her friend's kind wishes blest. He tasted in
The soothing draughts she gave, her mingled sweets
Of soul, and drank affection, full of hope,
In every drop that 'suaged his pains.

        So, as
Time roll'd on, Athol's frame evinced contempt
Of death ; and, ere a month elapsed, the tide of
Life, full high, in the crooked channels of his veins,
Return'd its purple flood. Restored at last,
He from his ailing couch arose, renewed
In lease of days and years, quite sound in health,
In spirits buoyant ; but with a sensation
In his heart unfelt ere he became thus
Convalescent. A sacred charm it was ;
Supremely divine ; so soul entrancing ;
But quite mysterious in its strange effects
Thro' all his being : but especially,
Did young Athol, when his benefactress

Stood, so kind, so fair and pure before him,

With her brow serene as the effulgent moon

Beaming down thro' Heaven's blue dome, keenly

Feel, in his warm heart, that inward pleasure.

Was it the grateful services, which in

His hours of sickness, her gentle hand had

Render'd? that which, day after day, he blest?

The one, which from the cold damp ground, had

    raised

His drooping head and bound with fingers fair

His wound? which smoothed his pillow? which

    prescribed,

In that propitious hour, the remedy

Whose potent agency within his frame,

Made his soul feel loath to leave its feeble house

Of clay, that caused the glow within his breast?

Was it her graceful form and beauty rare?

Her dulcet voice that softly syllabled

Sweet Bible stories, and sang in accents

Toned divinely, choice psalmody, which had

In Athol's hours of fevered sleeplessness lull'd

His throbbing brain to rest ? or was it the power

Of Daisy's pity, that in Athol's heart,

Had softly struck the mute accord of

Sympathy divine ?

Such, in truth, it was ;

For the compassion of his cherubim had

In his heart enkindled the pure flame of

Love : for gratitude begets love ; and when both

Are happily in women's heart combined,

What panacea so potent to remove

The anguish'd bosom's pain, to raise the head
    weigh'd

Down with cares, and solace give unto life's woes?

Athol, then, the more he saw the maid, became

Enamored with her sprightly comeliness ;

With her spirit beneficent, and with

The beam celestial which sparkled brightly

In the light blue eyes of Daisy : for he saw
The beam of truth in her heart illumed
Her cheeks with virtue's flame. In her presence
He would quite forget his past disaster,
And seldom thought that he had peril'd death
Upon the field of slaughter, so overjoyed
Was he, that he felt he could in seas of
Carnage wade, aye, a thousand dangers brave,
To pin so fair a jewel to his heart,
And keep the precious treasure there for life.

So, thus, while the maid in Athol's bosom
Was the only bliss ; the only vision that
Beguiled his mind ; the sole angel who came
To cheer him in death's dread hour : his treasure
Rarest that moved his bosom with the throb
Of fond affection. Daisy, herself, felt swayed
By some resistless influence in his soul.
'Twas the same power which she'd infused in his
     heart,
That in her own rebounded, and there found

Its sweet abiding place ; strange affinity

That tied their two souls with dearest amity :

For the more he amended, the more she droop'd.

Alternate gay and pensive were her looks.

Her languishing mien evinced her heart was

Fraught with love, which Athol saw and heard
   breathe

In her tender sighs ; and knew her condolement

Was the purest emblem of a constant mind ;

That her modest sweetness showed her virgin
   soul :

And that, although her tongue was then too coy

To breathe the tender vow, yet her silence

Was but the dumb rhetoric of her heart,

More eloquent of love than her sweet tones could
   lisp.

His fond gaze likewise made her looks obey

Her passion's impulse, burning in her heart,

So fervently ; as it summoned the blush,

Which her chaste bosom wore, to carminate,

As like a peach's rind, her modest cheeks.

7

'Twas thus that her affection for Athol
Her affliction became ; for, when he had
Recovered to that normal state which makes
Health laugh at death, she leaner grew, and
    proved,
By her pallor and sigh spontaneous,
The hidden pow'r which he exerted o'er her.
To him, in short, a thousand nameless actions,
Spoke the evidence of a tender wound
In her breast.   Thus did the dominant passion
That sways the world entire, enchain the hearts
Of both the rescued and the rescuer.

CHAPTER V.

The Lovers—The Vow—The Adieu—The Storm—
The Guerillas—The Altercation.

ONE bright morn as the lovers near the cot
Breathed forth their vows, Athol, in his own, took
Daisy's hand, and pressed it tenderly ; drew

Her to his breast and sigh'd within her ear
The ardent nature of his love.   Pallid
Spread her rosy cheeks. She trembled, and 'gainst
Her restraint, hung down her head in silence.
Athol, whose heart was full, stood mute awhile.
He scarce knew what to say, and deeply sigh'd :
But dared at length his passion to reveal.
He told her that he much admired her from
The time her eyes first on him gazed, and that
He then adored her fondly, so much so,
A king his bliss might envy ; that, if she were
His own, a soldier's and a lover's soul
She'd crown ; that when his term of service ended,
He'd hail her as his future bride ; united,
Blest with her, in bitter winds of winter,
And in snow's incessant fall, in ev'ry
Vernal hour he'd with her live forever,
Her heart's true partner.

             Now, what a shock was
That to one whose bosom was susceptible

And tender; soon her head reclined all
Pensive, which betrayed that something undefined
Was working in her mind.   Some affliction
That spoke her sadden'd thoughts, tho' mute her
    voice.
In that still mood, she seem'd so like a bird
Allured, pent up in a cage with her captor
Near her, enamored, patiently gazing,
And awaiting its dulcet strains to hear.
As he then did the sanction of her smile.
So, in brief time, from his panting heart, she
Raised her drooping head, and with her face
Upturned, threw her radiant eyes, bedimm'd with
    tears,
Full on his own.

            She told him that 'twere worse
Than death from him to part ; that a prey she'd
Be to separation's pain and sorrow ;
That none could comfort her but him ; then said :
" Alas! when thou art gone, foul darkness will
            7*

Be seen where once thy lightsome footstep shone."
Then she hinted fears that, he now being well,
Would forever leave her in affliction,
And bade him, strenuously, to stay with her,
Where peace and undivided love reposed.

But when Athol heard her fear-fraught words, he
Swore he'd never from his plighted faith depart :
That sacred was his word : his mind too pure
And high : his heart too merciful and just ;
In short, an honorable youth he was,
And loath'd the very name of infamy :
That naught within the wide world could seduce
Him from her, from truth, nor rectitude.
Then he told her that, although he'd suffer'd
From an outward wound—a bloody gash, that
He then suffer'd from an inward pang,
A heart-bruise deep, which naught could heal save
      but
Its kind :—" the tyrant god which thro' the world

Roams free, and robs its victims of their peace

And liberty."

Then Daisy looking up

With aspect mild, all inexpressive grace,

Her countenance beaming with approving smiles,

Which showed that Athol had with tones un-

daunted

Sued her not in vain, gladly promised

To commit her hand forever to his trust.

Athol then upon the head of his betrothed

Called Heaven's blessings down, and sealed his faith

With kisses on her dimpling cheek ; gave her

From vest pocket, his own portrait color'd,

Which she kissed with ardor sweet, and said; "ah!

Thy much-loved image, Athol, in my heart shall

Be enshrined, by friendship guarded until

Life is gone, as I feel assured thou hast

Indeed an upright heart, a fervent soul,

And temper gen'rous—jewels which fame nor

Gold can buy."

So, when the sullen clouds of doubt

Flit from her mind, hope's bright sunshine Daisy's

    thoughts

Illumined and stamped its vignette bloom upon

Her cheeks. With unmixed ardor in her heart

She hailed the joyous day when hand in hand

Together she would with her Athol walk

On sunny paths, and rove in vernal meads,

Where birds and bees and flowers the light obey,

And to their happy sights their silken plumes

Disclose. For, then, no frowning clouds she

    thought

Were in the sky, ominous of fortune's wrath,

Would cause a tear of agony to start from

Out her gladsome bosom ; that no lightning

Would flash and strike the bliss from out their

    barque

Of hope, while tossing to and fro on life's

Tempestuous billow.

    'Twas then the noontide hour.

The fluid gold of light down from its throne

Of blue began to sickly gleam upon

The mountain's slope, as Athol stood prepared

Upon the cottage steps to take his leave.

In tearful eyes, the old folks held him by

The hands ; and much regretted that they were,

So soon, deprived of their companion—

Their dear daughter's choice,—and welcomed him

    again,

If saved while warring with his brethren 'gainst

Traitors armed in his own country of birth.

Told him, too, that if he'd fall defending

His dear native land, they'd bless his name ; but

Hoped that God would spare him.

                Then Daisy flung

Her arms around his neck, and clinging to him

Prayed, as on he moved to go, that for the love

Of God and her he'd soon again return.

But, while Athol on the door-step stood wiping

From his humid eyes, the parting tear, he saw

The sunbeam from the casement faded fast,

And heard afar deep-noised rumbling thunder ;

Saw the distant light grow faint and sombre ;

And, hov'ring in the west, that thick, dark clouds

Announced a hostile sky ; that a storm was

Gathering.   Still his ardor was undaunted :

He cared not for the thunder's angry voice,

But wish'd to hasten thither on his journey,
To report at Washington for duty.

But just as he pronounced the farewell word
"Adieu," unusual darkness o'er the face
Of nature spread.   A vivid flash lit up
The gloom.   On through the immeasurable void

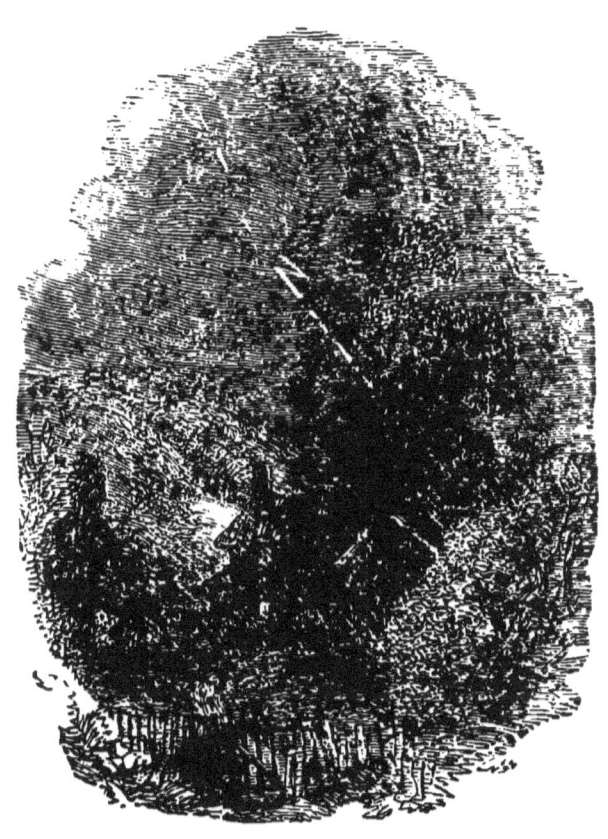

Of air, the war of elements roared and made
The welkin ring tremendously.—A flash—
A rattle,—down burst clouds of drenching rain.—
Fiercely howled the wind among the trees ; they
 groan'd—
Strained heavily and rustled off their leafy pride :
But a gust still more powerful wrenched from
Its roots an agèd oak which grew hard by.
The crash, the old man startled to his feet.
Quickly he ran to the window to see
The damage done, when in a glaring sheet
Of vivid lightning which just then illumed
The dark profound, his quick eye saw, along
The hillside, a troop of mounted horsemen
All drenched unto the skin, slowly wending
Their way onward to'ards the cot.

      Foremost in
The van, a stately creature tower'd, bedecked
Full proud in coat of grey all button'd up
But somewhat faded ; for, its nap appeared

As if it had seen many dreary seasons.

Armed he was from the saddle to his teeth

With revolvers three, a sabre, carbine,

And a dirk, showing what a monster of

War and human blood was he ; and the eye

That fiercely rolled beneath the knitted brow

Of this rough type of man, plainly showed

He was both bloody and remorseless

At his trade.   His nag, likewise, looked mean,
    spare,

Not half fed ; and its hide and harness was

With mud and grease and lather much befouled.

Soon at the cottage door the guerilla

Pranced his jaded steed, and deigned to knock.
    The noise

Of such a rap unusual startled all

The inmates to their feet at once.   Quickly

The daughter to the door hasten'd, and with

A curt'sy low and smile serene, welcomed

From the fitful wind and rain, the stranger.

The inmates all, save Athol, looked amazed
Upon his gaudy form, from the knee-top boots
He wore, to his slouch hat by tassel girt.
Then soon, kind Reuben's liberal hand took
By the reins, the fellow's neighing palfrey,
And tied it to a hickory post close by.
As kindly, the matron spread before him
A meal, of which he heartily ate, eyeing,
In the meanwhile, the federal youth disguised,
Whom he pierced, as 'twere intuitively.

So, when the chief his appetite appeased,
He hit upon a theme to drag to light
The truth he thought in Athol lay concealed.
"Kind friends of peace," he said, "I humbly thank
You. May your happy lives, unsullied
Flow down the stream of time, free from care and
    pain.
May good health your daily walks attend,
And cheerfulness sit smiling on your brows."
At this, all but Athol him their thanks return'd.

"Think not, my friends," he said, "that I speak
In this vein to curry favor.   No, I'm
Quite averse to flatt'ry, yet ne'er displease ;
And have a soul too dignified to kneel
And servile bend for selfish motives.   These
My unobtrusive nature never has ;
For, truth I admire undisguised, and scorn
Concealment."   (Fixing his eyes on Athol.)
" Honest ambition is my only pride,
Which I hope to mark along with other
Valiant heroes, firm, proud, and defiant,
Who've joined the cause of right 'gainst usurp'd
      might,
Contesting every inch of Southern soil
Against the pilf'ring Yankees : those minions
Of that perjured hypocrite who now sits
Upon his abolition throne, awing
The vulgar North to his way of thought, while,
We of the South brand him with contempt and
      hate,
And spurn his mean authority.   Tisn't
                    7*

The nature of the Southern heart to crouch

Before a tyrant. What! the pride and valor

Of the chivalry cringe to an uncouth

Abolitionist. What humiliation!

All of us would rather see the fruitful South

One vast wilderness. Aye, e'en suffer death,

Extermination first, before we'd stoop

To his yoke. No, the people South are bound

As one huge bulwark of strength to defend

Themselves to the last man against his sway ;

Till freedom's banner, the stars and bars, shall

Wave triumphantly o'er every State in

The Confed'racy."

                        Then Athol to his feet

Arose and cast upon the rebel braggart

A contemptuous sneer, and said with warmth :

    " Sir,

The honor'd President elect whom you've   ·

Deprecated vilely, is one of

The greatest men of modern times. Fate, once in

A thousand years, scarce gives us such a man.

The mental calibre that he's got

Rarely springs from out the dross of earth, to show

The world Heaven's model of a statesman.

With such a giant intellect possess'd,

He'd rise in any sphere of life and shine ;

As the aids which humbler minds require he

    scorns.

Being a ripe scholar, a sage, and wit, but

No pedant ; no display he makes of what

His mind contains.   He's too retiring, meek,

Timid, and, I may say, bashful, to parade

His learning.   Such modesty feeble minds

May despise ; but it shows *his* profound sense,

And proves he has a cultivated mind.

Nor pomp of speech has he, the ignorant

To dazzle, the weak dismay : his words are

In the simplest garb arrayed, and full of

Thoughts pregnant with truth and wisdom.

Yet, sometimes, I'll admit, that when he feels

In playful humor and an auspicious chance

Prompts its display, he'll tell a good joke ;

But, otherwise, he's a man of feeling ;

His heart is full of pity for his kind ;

So tender at times that his sympathies

Towards the human race are so great, they cause

His bosom pain ; and what you call tyranny,

Is nothing more than his firmness with which

He guides the Senate and rules the States.   In
    short,"

Continued Athol, "his name is cherished

In ev'ry loyal heart, who, at his voice

Commanding them, pour out their blood and
    treasure

In streams abundant, with which triumphant yet

He'd crush the lawless spirits now rampant

In the trait'rous South ; and I, as one, have,

At the just call of his great mind, resigned

Both health and ease, and will lay down my life

Itself an hostage on the bloody field,

To disenthrall the enslaved, and liberate

The free from the fangs of your cruel chief,

Who, both white and black, now holds in
bondage,
Ruling and ruining them remorselessly."

Indignant wrath then burned in Athol's blood.
He dared, scoffingly, his manly spirit
To unfold, and, unrestrained, continued :
"But we'll yet lower the lofty pride of
That pusillanimous puke, and drive him
To the verge of hell, where fiery dragons
Him will sting to death, ere his guilty soul
Falls in the flames, to writhe in tortures there
Forever with the damn'd, for urging, with
His barb'rous will, millions to fell slaughter."

This roiled the rebel's temper. He, angry,
Made with his clench'd fist a thrust at Athol,
Who dext'rously warded off the blow ;
Then to the door ran, with mouth all foaming
With rage, and shouted to his armed band,
"Foes—

Enemy—hither hasten—quick." Soon they
The house surrounded, hooted, halloo'd, rushed
Through the door, and like hungry tigers, pounc'd
Quite furious on their prey.

Then all within
The cot was dire confusion. Bitterly
The mother and the daughter wailed. Morose,
The guerilla chief jerked the old man up
Off his knees, and "villain, traitor," term'd him.
While with abject mien and supplication low,
Reuben tried to melt the chieftain's callous heart,
And bade him listen ere he claim'd him : raised
His eyes up heav'nward, and told him he was
Innocent : implored his freedom to restore.
While, meantime, Daisy wrung her hands with
    anguish :
In mercy lifted up her voice on high :
Bent her knees, and murmuring, bade him spare
Her father's hoary head : to be merciful
And just for the sake of her dear mother,

Stricken down with age, who, if of her spouse

Bereft, wouldn't live to see the morrow's light,

As God would call her from life's checquered

    scenes.

"Thou hast the power to wound or heal, to blight

Or bless :" but all was dead and still about

The chieftain's heart—too callous and to all

The finer feelings cold.   Nor even could

The nervous tremor of her hands, that clasp'd

His knees, vibrate soft pity to his heart.

Nor her sighs, nor tears, nor accents tender,

Nor e'en the melting sweetness of her eyes,

Nor their fascinating gaze, from which the heart

Of one less hard would sure destruction found.

All her pleadings were, alas! in vain ; as

The bold ruffians, in the remnant of the storm,

Quickly bore their captives from the vale, and
    thrust

Them in a loathsome dungeon South.

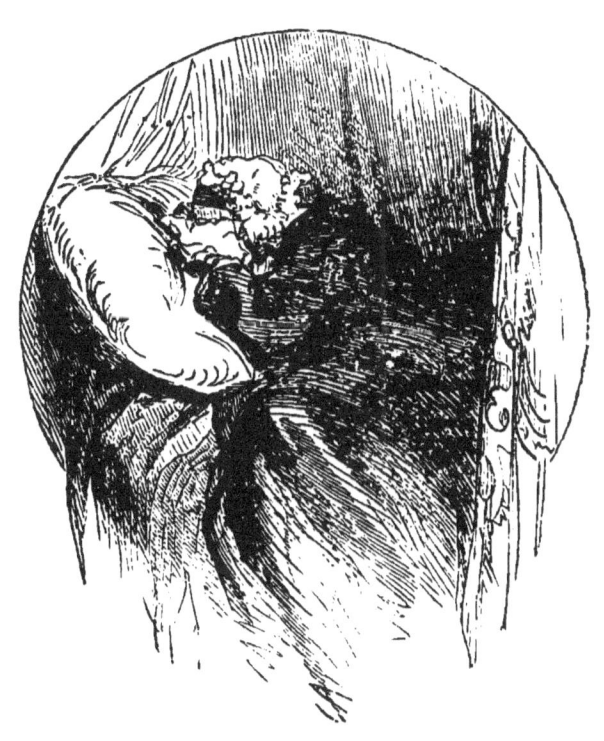

CHAPTER VI.

The Affliction of Daisy—The Death of both her
Parents.

Down beside her senseless mother Daisy

Knelt, and loudly called to Heaven for justice ;

Pour'd forth in fervent pray'r that mercy yet

Divine might smooth the captives' way—vain hope.

9

Bitterly, all that long and dreary night,

She wept her father's and her lover's hapless fates ;

And when the next day serenely dawn'd,

It brought unto her mind no smiling light,

For, joyless all the live-long day, she thought

Of them o'erwhelm'd by tyranny :

Knelt, with her heart o'ercharged with woe, and
  pray'd

The right'ous soon would triumph o'er and sink,

To fathomless depths, their stern oppressors down ;

Hop'd that they'd by divine vengeance be pursued ;

That the wrath of Heaven would upon them

Hurl its thunderbolts and doom their overthrow ;

Wish'd her aged father would again be

Free as the rolling cloud, enjoying once more

The blessings of liberty ; and that the wind

From heaven, unconfined, would soon play round

Her lover's brow, to dare again the foe,

Till vict'ry crown'd his arms, and conquest, with

Renown, his freedom brought. For she knew her

Athol's noble heart was far too valiant

To shrink from treason-tainted foes ; aye scorn'd

At danger ; could hear taunts and wear his chains

In fetter'd realms like a Christian martyr.

But such hopes her mother's mind relief denied :

Soon reason fled her fever'd brain ; for when

By her injurious foes borne down, faint she

Lay outstretch'd, pale nigh breathless, upon

A bed of anguish.

                            Many nights Daisy

Watch'd with glistening eye around her couch ;

And heard, in her mother's stifling moans, death,

In fullness of glee, with bony hands twang'd

At her heart-strings, the solemn tones which tell

Where the broken in spirit shall go.   Yes,

The tale is told : hopeless of recovery

Was her state ; for soon her weaken'd lungs closed

Their spongy cells against the air of life.

A sigh, a gasp, a rattle in her throat :

Her fitful struggles ceased, and all was still.

Her spirit fled its earthly confinement,
And soared far beyond life's narrow bounds.

If ever innocence knew distress 'twas when
Daisy, bending o'er her dying parent,
Heard her last breath, and felt her heart was reft
Of life's warm beat.   In her deep despair she
Trembling knelt beside her deceased mother ;
And from her weeping eyes she pour'd upon
Her cold remains many fond, filial tears.
Then she raised her sorrowing head on high,
And cried aloud : "To thee, Great God above, let
My imploring voice ascend.   O Lord of
Mercy ! hear my prayer.   Thou hast the power
To raise or quell the storm.   The struggling worm
Thou canst protect.   Then, O Lord of Hosts !
    deign
To dispel the black'ning gloom which now
    o'ershades
The future of a helpless orphan just
Deprived of fond maternal care.   Her voice

That once impressed celestial precepts on
My heart, is hush'd in death. Nor does my father
Hear his suppliant child beseeching Thy
Benign protection : for, far from me, alas !
He has been cruelly torn, and futile have,
I fear, his claims for mercy been ; unfelt
On apathetic hearts his pleading soft :
Still hearing naught but insults vile, has sank
Beneath oppression's weight ; and p'rhaps his
    soul
Has from its earthly cell been disencumber'd,
And upward wing'd its way to heaven for peace,
Leaving me an orphan here forlorn, the sole
Survivor of the wreck."

                                    Too true, alas !
Was her prediction : for, unhappily,
In mouldy dungeon vilely smear'd with
Damps infectious, her father, hopeless, sleepless,
Many midnight hours, quickly pined beneath
His darksome prison roof ; and while he droop'd
                    9*

And lonely breath'd, despairing of each daylight's
    dawn,
He thought that safe, secure, tho' far away,
All whom he loved remain'd in sunshine bright.

    He saw his white-washed cot, and the tall trees
Which rose above it proudly, tinted with
The beam.   Heard the gurgling brook meand'ring

Past ; and fancied, in its twirling eddies,

That he saw the trout disport : his daughter,

Too, quite fair ; serene as mild mid-noon in

Mayday, sitting on its green bank twining

A wreath of flow'rets gay with which to crown

Her lover's honored brow, in token of

The laurel he might wear.

      But yet, he knew,

The Fed'ral then with circling arms did not

Her slender bosom twine, as, like himself, he pined

In dungeon deep, in sad captivity,

Inly mourning the loss of her whom his soul

Loved best on earth.

      Then forebodings sad soon

Banish'd from his mind the remember'd joys

That thronged upon his soul. He feared and wept

To think that both his wife and child suffer'd :

Yet still at intervals he felt consolement

In the thought that they unshared his woes.

 Hoped

And prayed that no dire ills hung o'er their heads,

And that his wife and lovely daughter solely

Mourn'd his loss of fondness. This 'twas that cheer'd

Him ; for a degree of bliss he felt in

His heart that he might see them soon again.

'Twas but a mock'ry of joy, as forced was

The glow ; ghastly the smile ; his haggard cheeks

And hollow eyes that hope destroyed.   For, fast
He sank : and, on the self-same night his wife's
Christian spirit fled into eternity,
Death freed Reuben from his clanking chains.

CHAPTER VII.

The Funeral of Daisy's Mother—The Strange Visitor.

THE decease of Daisy's mother caused among
The neighbors of the vale a holiday
Of grief.   Promptly, the solemn call of death
Brought them to the cot where they found Daisy,
With a heavy load in her once lightsome heart,
Sadly bending her lithe form gently o'er
The unconscious relic of her parent.

As she her drooping head raised up to greet
Them, they saw how changed was the gay flower,
How withered in its charms ; how doleful, too,
Was her low voice that once rang through the
    meads
As cheer'ly as the morning bird's : whilst she,
With tearful eyes, the tale to them rehearsed

How of father, mother, lover, robbed by
A band of ruthless foes, who scorned to listen
To her voice that sued for mercy, but mock'd
Her heart so rent and sorely vexed with their
Injustice.

Some with their indignant tongues
Branded them with the foul names of scoundrel,
Churls, and tyrants cruel ; whilst others 'mong
The band of mourners who had their feelings
Touched, unrestrainedly, their sister streams
Of pity commingled with those of Daisy.

Then, as with one voice, they all together
Offered her sweet friendship's balm to solace
The repining sorrow that preyed upon
Her heart.

She sigh'd and thank'd them as they all
Around her mother's bier in solemn pray'r
Familiar knelt : and when the funeral rite,

Impromptued from the lips of a rough peasant,
Was ended, silently and slow the corpse
Was borne along a wild landscape and laid,
Down in its narrow bed, dug in a mound
Which nature made.

There, at her mother's shrine,
'Neath a cypress, whose sombre branches waved
With sympathetic sorrow o'er the rude slab
Which mark'd her earthly resting place, Daisy,
In the evening starlight, many a silent hour
Would sit and watch the clouds of autumn roll,
And tell to the passing winds in broken sighs,
The death of father, mother, and the loss
Of love and friendship, that undiminished
Yet burn'd in her lamp of hope, fed by the beam
Of faith and truth's undoubted ray.

Yet, at times,
She feared her own death would, ere long, com-
plete

The scene ; for, in her breast she felt a cipher

Writ that soon her earthly form she'd yield up

To the God of nature, to undergo

Creation's change : as the blighting grief

In her heart she felt, was too deep for the rose

On her cheek to re-blossom more.

"But why

Regret," she said, "Heaven may yet send me

A cup of sweet relief, consecrated

By faith, to guide my inexperienced youth

Thro' life's thorny ways.   Does not the author

Of life and death dispense with righteous hands

To his poor creatures, bliss or pain, as best

Befits them ?   Surely, then, I should my lot

Endure without repining : for metals

Are with red heat refined and freed from dross.

In affliction's burning furnace our souls

Are purified ; and if we can resist

Temptations, which are but the devil's tricks

To wean us from the Lord, why, surely, futile

10

Then must be ev'ry alluring guise
The tempter wears to snare us from the path
Of virtue, and blot out the good resolves
That love for the All-powerful once hath
Fixed within the heart.

         In her breast these truths
She recorded, then from her pale hands raised
Her head and wander'd to the blest retreat,
The chosen spot of love ; for Athol's nature
At her heart-strings yet unalt'rable play'd.

"Ah! here alas! how often have our hearts
With mutual endearment entwined, our hands
United fondly.   O hapless object
Now of my distress, thou art, perchance, long
Since number'd with the good. Aye, mute thy
     tongue
That softly sung of love. Yet, p'rhaps, thou liv'st in
Prison languishing, but wearing out thy chains
With hope and fortitude.   Ah! Athol dear,

Tho' mountains and wide-spreading plains divide

Us, still I boast a priv'lege, a dear one :

Fancy wafts me to thy arms.   Yet, oh ! if thou

Wert here, how much lighter would my burdens be."

Such were the thoughts sad Daisy spoke, while
    gazing

O'er the fair scenes of soft delight, where

At the sequester'd spot she linger'd till

The evening's breeze in fitful·gusts began

To moan among the leaves, and mountain clouds

Around the place a dusky shade diffused.

Thus night being close at hand, dispelled from

Her mind the train of placid thoughts and warn'd

Her hence.

    Soon upon the breeze she heard the tramp

Of horse—affright'd ran—reach'd the cot—turn'd
    round,

And saw a shadowy form hard by, hovering

Near.   Quick the door she shut ; but soon a rap

Vibrated on her startled ear.   Trembling,

She thro' the window gazed alarmed, and thought
She saw the chieftain returned back to burn
The cot, as twilight shadows veil'd the man,
And made his garb appear like gray.

                      Now listen
To her mind by prudence temper'd, her caution
Spoke with earnest warmth. "Who in evening's
    mantle
Sombre wrapt comes here ?" "A friend," was the
    response.
"A friend, forsooth ! at such an hour ! Perchance
A foe, as none but the intrusive would
Invade a lonely maiden's sanctuary :
None but the designing prowl about in
Gloomy shades of night, dark deeds to do,
In order that their evil work may the
Mortal eye elude, and you seemed fashioned
For no good intent."
                  "Call not suspicion
To your mind, lone maid ; I'm not on mischief

Bound.   Heaven is my witness.   My mission

Is a holy one, and needs precaution.

To guard against impending ills I must

Shun the cheerful beam of day, and wander

Only when the night shrouds the world in gloom.

The letter which I carry in my vest

Declares the object of my visit, and will,

I'm sure, remove your doubts : it's from Athol."

When she heard the gentle name of Athol,

She felt conscious that the stranger's ends were

Right ; and without further parley bade him

Enter.   Then he proffer'd her the letter,

Which she gladly took, and turn'd it round and
     round.

Her bosom heaved convulsed with deep emotion,

The sudden chill of fear quit her blood,

And stay'd the with'ring grief that blanch'd her
     cheeks

With paly dye, and sooth'd her thorny pains.

Then while Daisy, in the dim twilight, cast

A joyous look upon its superscription,

The stranger saw how beauteous was the maid,

How serenely fair in ev'ry feature.

Then, with the light of new-born hope, she from

The folded letter raised her languid eyes,

And said : "Tho' the lines seem to have been
  penn'd
By a trembling hand, yet I can trace in
Them the ornate style of dear Athol ; and may
Fate charter freedom's blessings to the brave
Who brought them.   May ev'ry adversity
Give him renew'd courage, till his name shall
Be upon the rolls of fame enshrined, and
Honors, like his days, brighten full of years."
The stranger bow'd his grateful thanks.

                              " How was
Dear Athol when you saw him last," she said.
" In health and hope quite buoyant ; for, to me,
His confidant, he often speaks of you
As being far above all mortal stars
That shine.   My praises, too, with his can now
Be joined."   Concluding which, Daisy look'd
  straight
At the stranger, and caught the quick glance of
His eye, but in it saw he was sincere :

Then, gently curtseyed at the flatt'ring words
Which he had spoken.

            "Most loth am I, fair maid,
To bid you now farewell ; but the pale star
Of eve shoots down its lustre, and shame might
Tinge your cheeks if here I tarried longer."
" O, sir," she said, "my tongue hath not power
Of words to tell the emotions that now
I feel : But give Athol this token of
My love, and murmur in his ear these vows
Of mine : Tell him that, 'so long as time shall
Last, his image will remain and still be
Cherish'd at my faithful heart, and that, like
The stream near which he's now encamp'd, my
    love
For him is deep and pure.' "

                  Delighted with
The kindly. task enjoined, the courier
Promised faithfully her commands he would

Obey.   Then both their hands in friendship's grasp
Were soon combined.

Hastily forth he sallied,
And nimbly mounted on his roan steed,
Which restlessly on the emerald sward paw'd
The deep green grass.   "Adieu," he said.   "Good
  bye "
"And may kind Providence guard you safely
On your way," was her response.   Then quickly,
The horseman and his charger, to her sight
Were lost, in the gloom of night enshrouded deeply.

CHAPTER VIII.

Athol's Letter to Daisy—She Quits her Place of
Birth—Her Search of Athol—Her Despair—
The Loyal Peasants—The Guerillas—
The Burning Hut—Its Victims.

In the calm silence of that evening hour,
As Daisy sat musing o'er the joyful news
Which Athol's letter might contain ; the moon,
Hastening from her eastern bowers, full flushed
Arose and brightly shone o'er all the vale ;
Glanced radiantly a trembling ray of light
Upon the cottage window.

                 A welcome boon
Was the refulgent beam to Daisy :
For, soon with cheeks by joy's warm glow suffused,
She fondly pressed the letter to her lips,
And, then, by love's pure torch read these words :

"In the field, near Philomont, Virginia,
"August 23, 1862.
"DEAR DAISY :—
"Although tyrant rapine hath
Reft me from thee, nor time, nor distance, nor
The hard severities which fate compels
Me to endure, hath blurr'd the impressions
Which thy dear love hath made upon my heart.
For when my mind on thy fond image dwells,
Cheerfully I bear my aches and pains and
Meet the dull monotonies of camp life.
Amidst all the hardships incident
To a soldier, and my perils on the field,
The heart-melting ecstasy still burns
In my breast, that I shall soon again see
Her whom my fond heart passionately adores.
Be then thyself thus warm with hope : for, in
Grief or absence, Heaven's just hand weighs well
The lot of human life.   Neglect no means
Which may be best to mitigate your pains ;
And when this inhuman conflict's o'er

And the last battle shall have been fought and
    won,
And death thro' ev'ry danger hath my life
Preserved, the black'ning clouds which now veil
    our
Hopes will have cleared away and then we'll bask,
Unrestrained, in the sunshine of love, till
Death puts an end to all our earthly joys.

  "But God alone knows when the feast of car-
    nage
Will be o'er, as the giant North, firm in
Her strength and lavish with abundant means,
Still pours forth, in myriads strong, new heirs
To glory. Therefore, blood must yet be bought
With blood ; for' unavailing thus far hath
Proved the threats of laws and force of arms
To quell the civil hate and strife. Ruin
Yet rolls its sweeping tide of misery along
Virginia's blood-stained fields, where, mingling
Their lamentations with the woundeds' groans,

Houseless are many old and young, besides
How much of woe unseen, how much untold.

"Even while I pen these lines, the news hath
Reached me that the self-same subtle fiend who
Has been the cause of all your wrongs, now
Leads a ruffian guerrilla gang through
The gorges of the Blue Ridge, to forage
In the plains of ill-fated Maryland ;
To steal horses, pasturing herds, and grain,
From the husbandmen : and p'rhaps, as they
        through
The Shenandoah pass, the marauders
Will pillage, burn, and make your rich valley
One devastated waste.   But rest assur'd
That all their agencies of hell will not
Our vigilance oppose.   We now sleep upon
Our arms, ready at a moment's warning
To rise combined as one to check their course.

"But if the lurking rebel should evade
Our watchfulness, in friendly guise he may

In all his pompous pride come to the cot

Again, and evermore darken the light

That beams in thine eyes so blue.   Consequently,

Forego no merit of good intent,

But rather seek safety in flight : as 'tis

Always best to fly when arm'd dangers threaten

Unarm'd innocence. Therefore, be on your guard :

The rest I'll leave to your own sagacious heart.

" ATHOL."

"May bliss from heav'n around thee dwell.   To
        see

Thee soon, dear Athol, I'll try.   Aye, even

Before the glowing sun to-morrow doth

Shine in the meridian, I will be on

My lonesome way.   Then quick, O smiling morn

Awake, that I may go in search of him who'll

Find my heart as firm, as pure and holy

As his own.   But if I should find him not—"

Here awhile she paused—then said : " Why
        then I'll

Weep him dead." Just then a fleeting cloud roll'd
Athwart the moon, and wrapt both her and earth
In the opake shroud of night.

                            Then sleep, with
Her bland Morphean folds, her heavy eyes soon
Sealed in soft repose, where, deep in dreamland's
Magic bowers, she lay unconscious but a spell,

For broken was her rest, which made the night

So long and irksome seem, that soon she from

Her restless couch arose, listen'd, but heard

No sound save the sigh of the low breeze.

Then casting up an anxious eye toward

The orb-bespangled crown of night, she saw

The paly lustre of the morning star

Faded languidly before the gleam of

Breaking day, which, afar upon the peaks

Of the high distant hills, shone tremblingly.

Then in her satchel dainties few she pack'd

For life's support, and cheering succour by

The way, where'er she'd shape her course, o'er hill,

Thro' grove, down dale. But yet, at first, too weak

Her resolution seem'd to quit her place

Of birth, and where her parent lay

In rude grave : for alone to leave the grave

Neglected, would evince no longer love

Nor filial duty.   Thus was her mind sway'd

By the fond pow'r of attachment.

At length
Reason came to her aid.   Loose purpose might
Lead to life's disgrace, and to linger there
Was to be undone. She shudder'd at the thought,
And said, she'd put her trust in Him who grants
Or takes away ; would go wherever fate
Or fortune her might waft ; and then, with fixed
Resolve, forth in the noontide beam she went
Where her dear mother's dust reposed, and there
  pluck'd
Off the grave a reed that trembling grew :
Then turn'd her fair face to'ards her childhood's
  home
She loved, and casting one last look upon
Her mother's blest abode, she, weeping, dash'd
Into a wood.

There her startled eyes peer'd
Round and round.   Thick incumbent shadows
  scowl'd
About her.   Ev'ry now and then she fear'd
11*

Some beast of prey would pounce upon and eat

Her.   But on she rov'd o'er plains and forded

Unknown floods.   Her bed sear'd leaves of
    autumn ;

Her pillow some bleak rock.   Nor fear then
    blanch'd

Her care-worn cheeks ; for the first tremor long

Since vanish'd from her breast.   Fortitude

All her power of endurance had summon'd,

And arm'd her with fix'd resolution :

With which she heeded not the howling of

The tempest, the lightning's vivid glare,

Nor the pealing thunder's crash.

                        Yet one day,

As the sun declined, she, weary, languid,

Faint, within a silent shelter'd spot sat

Veil'd in gloom, and there of hope bereft, sigh'd

And said : " Alas ! nothing but thorns my way

Beset.   Want, woe, and strife my pilgrimage

Doth vex.   Fruitless my search hath been.   Way-
    ward

Still my destiny ; for it seems Heaven doth

Deny me the expected joy to heal

The gnawing smarts which my misfortunes bring.

Then if I'm doom'd to die, why not here in

This wild wood ; for my wearied soul I feel

Wants to be enchain'd no longer down to earth,

But yearns to soar to the blest abode where

Shines yon bright and happy star.

　　　　　　　　　　Gazing upward,
Her eyes then caught a light gleaming dimly
　　through
The umbrage of the wood.　Both hope and fear
Soon took the place of her despair.　She knew
Not whether friend or foe resided whence　　.
The glimmer faintly shone ; yet something innate
Panted at her heart that a lone maid would
There be welcom'd, and soon the spot she reached;
Found to her great joy, the light proceeded
From a peasant's humble habitation.

　　She knock'd the door.　The panel gave the
　　sound.
A female voice within demanded, "Who
Is there?"　"One whom the winds blow fierce
　　about ;
A poor exile who wanders far and wide,
Houseless, friendless, and forlorn," said Daisy.

The last word scarcely fell from her lips ere
The door wide open on its hinges swung.

Tenderly they mark'd her mournful mein,
And saw too well her sunken eyes exprest
The haggard sign that deep corroding care

Was eating up her mind : how faint she was
From hunger and her toilsome journeyings.

But soon they from their homely board bestow'd
On Daisy choicest fare—the gen'rous mite

Unask'd ; for, tho' scanty was the portion
Nature gave to them, yet they spared not when
The hungry craved, the houseless needed shelter ;
For they good-natured were, if not refined
With the gloss of worldly worth.   Charity
Comes from the soul : its promptings are divine ;
This Daisy knew, and estimated rightly
Their gen'rous hearts by what their hands had
    given.

   All amazed they listen'd to the story
Of her woes, and felt indignant at the deeds
The cruel rebel done, and him denounc'd
A brute.   Then she told them that 'twas fear
Which made her leave her native home, and
    love,
That sadden'd all her thoughts, to wander so
With beating heart and eager hopes to find
Her lover youth, a soldier brave, who gloried
To be foremost in the fight ; and tho' in
Many an adverse battle tried, yet smiled

On dangers past, and lived the open foe
Of traitors to their country.

Then she from
Her bosom Athol's vignette drew. They gazed
Admiringly upon his handsome face ;
But quickly alternating their delight,
With much surprise they said :

"Alas ! not long since
A squad of Fed'ral soldiers, arm'd with weapons
Of death, came down yonder mountain's steep,
Singing songs of freedom and strains of love.
Their leader's features strong resemblance bore
Unto this likeness, but more swarthy
His complexion seemed ; but this may have been
Caused by his exposure to the scorching sun.
Nor were his cheeks so round and full ; still,
This can be attributed to his love
And distant thoughts of you ; but his hair, like
This, was black as a raven's wing."

"Then fright,

Unknown before, seized our hearts, for 'twas

The first time that our wond'ring eyes ere saw

Men dressed up in clothes fantastic.   "Fear not,"

The leader said, " we are your friends : ours is

No hostile banner : it waves for freedom,

Law, and order, not for spoliation :

And on many a hard-fought field against

The foe it has been reared.   Therefore be not

Alarmed ; your lives are safe : no invaders

Now your quiet retreat explore."

"Thus he spoke,

Soft as the accents of a child, and yet,

As he turned round to face his men, I thought

I saw an insidious smile play round his mouth ;

Still we 'sposed they were sincere, that men train'd

Up to mortal combat, and who'd achieved

Heroic deeds whilst sternly battling with

Frantic hordes of lawless foes, surely would

Not stoop their honors to defame and blight.

The laurels they so nobly earned, to hurt

The harmless and injure the confiding.

But, alas! faithless were those friends : they
    proved

Themselves our greatest enemies ; for when

We gave them all the food and drink they
    needed ;

In short, to ev'ry one impartially

Our gen'rous care extended ; they, after

Partaking of our hospitality,

Stole from the plow my husband's oxen : took

My best two milch cows, then shot our poultry ;

And carried on their depredations till

Nearly all the means with which we life

Supported, they knavishly purloined.

"But mark, this is not all : the knaves added

Insult to injury ; for when we ask'd

Payment for the chattels which they'd stolen,

Harsh and rude the wretches laugh'd, and drove

Before them our sheep, horses, hogs, and cattle :

12

Ev'n now the thankless and irreverent tongues
Of the audacious roughs ring in my ears."

"Can aught in human nature be less kind?
Hard it is indeed to bear such wrongs," said
    Daisy,
"Yet none the less, my friends, have they, I find,
Subdued the gen'rous feelings of your hearts.
Bount'ous strangers, now farewell. Quick must I
Pursue my way, to resolve whatever
Fate decrees me."

        Just then appalling sounds
Of horror wild arose upon her ears. "Death
To foes : captivity to traitors : slaughter
And·slav'ry yet shall triumph." Daisy shrank
With fright, and cold sweat beaded on her brow.

Soon the same guerillas bold, with torches
In their hands, and with augmented force 'proach'd
    her.

She gave a piercing shriek and fainting fell

To earth.   "A female spy," the ruffians cried,

Then looking down they thought the damsel dead,

And raised her prostrate form up from the ground,

And bore her to a darksome glade hard by the hut.

Then back they to the cot their hasty steps

Retraced.   Their presence to the old folks' hearts

Wild terrors brought. Quick, the peasant pale with
Horror leaped from his bed and on his knees
Begg'd the rebels to spare the helpless lives of
Both himself and wife.

                    "Yes, we shall," they cried,
"If you own our sway, our cause defend, and leave
This place, wherein a moment since we saw
You aid and comfort give unto a foe."

But the peasant scorn'd to quit his home, and
        said :
"His constancy to his country was due,
And that he'd rather die than sell his birthright
To those who fought to oppress and conquer'd
To enslave."

                    This roused the rebels' ire.   They
Struck, then kick'd their kneeling foe.   For mercy
Pray'd the wife.   But her tears nor lamentations
Could melt their stony hearts.   Soon the cot

In burning ruins blazed.   Writhing hands rose

Up amid the sheeted flames imploring

The avenging angel down to hurl

Red bolts of wrath upon and strike the hearts

Of the inhuman wretches dead with fright.

While amid their last screams of agony

Were heard, "We treason hate, and traitors scorn;

True to the Union die—loyal to the last."

12*

CHAPTER IX.

Daisy a Captive—The Bivouac—Daisy's Doom.

Not till their victims' charr'd remains exhaled,
Through murky wreaths of smoke, a pestilence
Most baleful, did the rebels quit the hut
In search of injured Daisy, whom they found
Much convulsed and with all her sense nigh fled.

Through dark desert ways and rugged paths
    they,
Unmindful of her piteous cries, her sobs,
Her plaints and bitter wailings, brought her to
A cavern deep, scoop'd out between two hills,
And laid her in a dark recess wherein
Her fate should be determin'd by their chief,
Who'd not, as yet return'd.

                        So, round a blazing fire,

The murd'ring crew caroused. Some the weed
    fum'd.
Some sang ribald songs by turns and smutty jokes
Got off, whilst others quaffed and pass'd around
A vile inebriant distillation.

    "Drink, comrades, drink," more loquacious than

The rest, cried one. "Drain your canteens to the
    dregs.

'Tis the most potent of all drinks, to rouse

Our sluggish blood to life and fortify

Us 'gainst dangerous night damps.   Besides, it is

Our chieftain's birthday night.   Then let us all

Be merry, jocund, gay, and laugh at folly

As it flies on pleasure's wing.   For, why should

We work our own annoy, when now we have

A chance to pass a lucid interval

From a life attended with so many

Dangers ?   True, to lead this wild course has been

Our own choice ; or, rather, we were all forced

Into it by the roving propensities

Of our natures, and ungovernable wills

That could not bear restraints, nor drudgeries,

Nor the enervating dull routines of

The regular soldier.   No, my comrades ; among

These hills we are free to do what we please.

Here we can and do despise the outer world.

Where glaring vice and luxury prevail ;

Where laws are made most stringently to force

City villains into decency.

But here, full of adventurous love, among

These mountain passes, we simply practise

The ancient virtues of our ancestors,

With a valiant chief whose freeborn soul nought

Can turn from perilous ways; aye, one who spurns

The niggard Yankees' selfish yoke and hates

Their clannish, over-jealous natures. Still,

Sometimes when he's not aware, I notice

That his high-toned spirits are much dejected,

So much so, in fact, he seems to struggle

Against some opposing fate, the cause of

Which I opine I know. So, if you'll cease

Your drowsy murmurs, and open your ears,

I'll breathe into them, the sad incident

Of his life which yet preys upon his mind.

"Two years have scarce elapsed since he was
    smitten

With the peerless charms of a Yankee maiden

Whose father, a Puritan born and bred,

Lavish'd on her with unsparing hands,

The wealth he'd gain'd running niggers from

Africa into the Isle of Cuba,

Hoping, thereby, that his gifts of fortune,

Along with her accomplishments, would add

Great dignity to his high lineage ;

Grace the pious stock from which she sprang,

And draw around her swarms of wealthy suitors."

"Our noble chief, a Virginian by birth,

Was always at her father's house a welcome guest ;

For he thither often went to interchange

With her father mutual thoughts concerning

Their clandestine interests in the slave trade.

So, whilst in social converse, the father learnt

That Agar was descended from one of the

Eldest and most distinguished families

Of old Virginia.   Then coupling this news

With the proud notions of himself, he saw

That such high blood, with wealth united, would

Confer much honor on his house, and offer'd
Agar his daughter's hand in marriage,
With vested rights in estates as portion
Of her marriage dower.   Agar consented,
And promised to solemnize the nuptials
When he'd returned from Paris, where he'd gone ·
Some months before the war broke out.

But in
That gay city, where vice and shame strut round
Enrob'd in meek-sainted guise, wine and women
Soon his youthful bosom fired.   Held spell-bound
By the charming witch'ries of the gay lorettes,
Who hold their bacchanals at the Chateaux
Des Fleurs and Mabille, soon his unthinkin ʒ
And blind reason brought him down deep into
The gulf of dissipation, which soon made
Him needy ; for, amid his orgies, he thought
Not of the ruin he was bringing
On himself, but, to relieve his pressing wants,
Continued to make frequent demands

For means from her father, and gave his lands
In Virginia to him as surety
For supplies.

        " At last the day of reck'ning
Came. The Yankee complain'd of tardy payment ;
Felt touch'd to the quick in consequence,
And vouchsafed to lend our chief no more funds.

    " So, one bright morning, the captain awoke
To the consciousness that shadowy ills
Obscur'd his stores at home ; and once more.
        steer'd
His shatter'd barque across the ocean wave.
On arriving home he found his domains
Were laid waste by the war which fiercely raged
Upon his native soil, his slaves set free ;
In short, his happy home, and what remain'd
Of his once fair realms, confiscated were
By the Federal jackals.

"But yet his cup of

Mis'ry was not full : one drop it lack'd

More turgid still.   Adverse fate deign'd to add

Poignancy to his misfortunes : for with

Harsh disdain the maiden's father on him

Fix'd an eye malignant, and with anger

Bade him never more to cross his threshold.

"Struck with such unkindness, our chieftain

   took

It in his heart to loath forever more

The Yankees, and swore he'd hold dread reverence

O'er their heads, joined our cause, then took these

   hills

To—"

Awe-struck, they him beheld.   He came with

Hurried tread.   Amazed, he stood awhile as

If some boding ill gleam'd through his eyes.

Soon his abject crew bent to his pride, and quit

The bivouac his wishes to fulfill :

To forage round and ransack spots, which, in
Open day, their footsteps fear'd to tread.

   When gone, the ingrate bold the weak maid
      eyed
O'er and o'er ; gave her many a wishful look ;
And urg'd by lust, the leafy couch approach'd
On which she slumbering lay.   She started up
As from a trance, with hair dishevell'd much,
And features fix'd in stern expression wild,
And on him threw the keenest dart of scorn.

   Barb'rously severe he her accused of
Trait'rous complicity, and, indignant,
Said : "Haughty fair one, now thy doom's decreed.
Thou shalt have but one hour more to linger here,
If now thou dost not to my wishes lend
A gracious ear."

            Down on her knees Daisy
Look'd up at him with mild, imploring eyes,

And with anguish in her bosom, wailing,

Said : "Alas! he's thought severe who thus con-

demns

The innocent and unhappy. Hast thou

Not one friend to whom the sacred heart relies

For truth and honor ? If not, then such have

I—one ardent, noble, kind : In faith and hope

Unfaltering we are bound."

But her soft pleadings

Could not move his harden'd heart : It was bereft

Of all that's meek and tender. He heeded not

Her tears, her firm faith, nor virtue proud,

But said : "You'll never see your lover more.

In prison he now wears his chains. P'rhaps ere

Now, the Yankee's rotten carcase has been

To the buzzards thrown." "Then if Athol is

To me forever lost," she cried, "God bless

His soul. His image so dear to my sight shall

In my heart be firmly fixed, nor ever

From my cherish'd memory fade. But thou,

Vile minion of all that's mean and great,

The willing tool of that vain man whose pride

Is phrenzy, whose ambition's but despair,

Whose heart is void of ev'ry spark divine,

The curse of orphans and the cause of

Many a widow's tear, know that you may

Glitter in your infamy awhile ;

But the potent grasp of might shall be soon

Wrested from you : The majesty of pow'r

Is in the avenging sword held in the hand

Of Heav'n : 'twill yet descend upon and burst

Your vaunted bubble to the sun, aye, blast

Your lauded greatness : Deeds of retribution

Deal unto the mean and base ambitious fools

Upon the gibbet ; and righteous justice

Yet shall hurl upon thee its avenging ire,

For the wrongs which thou hast cruelly brought

Upon my Athol's hapless head : Aye, you

Who came into that happy home where dwelt

In blessed peace the innocent whose ears

Were strangers to the blast and din of war,

And vilely brought, therein, much misery,

Wretchedness and mourning.   My father's name

Blasphem'd with curses foul, then reft him from

Me, and in a dungeon dire, him thrust, to pine,

To starve, and die : my aged mother caused

Through pining grief to sink into her grave

Ere she'd time to don a widow's mourning weeds ;

And me an outcast orphan made for life.

But remember, yours is but a weak boast

Of transitory power.   Successful guilt

Can but triumph awhile :   For soon before

The keen, relentless weapons of the North,

Both your stuck-up pride and cause shall

Tumble : 'tis to them alone revenge is

Given.   Beware."

At this, in drunken fury,

The chieftain laugh'd outright, and said: "Murmur

Not, my dear, fond bird.   Do you think I'd injure

A bosom so fair.   Beauty like thine was

Form'd for joy ; and you must own I'm now

Your lawful lord."

        Then he strove with eager arms
To grasp her.   As quick she from his touch re-
   coil'd.
"Shrink not," he angrily cried.   "Succumb
To my power thou must, or, in this dense wood
Unseen by mortal eye, from life to death
Thou soon shalt pass ; for, longer my mind
Thy indiff'rence can't bear, thy peevish censures
Endure : nought but thy consent to be my bride
Can satisfy my burning soul."   Saying which,
He grasped her by her long dishevell'd hair.
"Swear," he cried, "ere this dagger's keen edge
   shall
In your heart's blood be imbrued."

        "No, no," she said,
"Fate will ne'er permit me to touch thy hand,
It hath the stain of murder'd blood ; and such love
As thine, the tender-hearted would defile :

Forever unhappy she'd be whose bosom

Hath therein sincere passion glowing. No,

My honor lives for one most dear to my heart.

Therefore, if my ardent troth for him I love

Can't kindle in thy breast compassion's warmth,

Why longer the sacrifice delay ? Why

Tantalize your victim like a cat ere

You destroy ? or like the venom'd adder

Coil your folds around ere you sting to death

Your prey ? For well I know he who would not

Spare my father's life will not spare my own ;

And death would end the tortures which now rack

My beating heart. But beware. He yet lives

For whom my soul with sacred fervor burns.

He whom thy bold hands hath sway'd with cruelty,

But who will yet thy proud triumph guilt

Avenge."

   Then reviving wrath the chieftain's soul

Inflam'd. The name of Athol moved his heart

To hate ; and black as night he frown'd and spent

His rage on helpless Daisy, who struggled

At his feet.   Her clasp'd hands clinging round his

    knees ;

With dripping eyes to Heav'n raised and crying,

"Oh! God of mercy! is there no friend nigh ?"

" There is a friend," a deep gruff voice behind

A rock exclaim'd.   "Arrogant knave, forbear."

The rebel heard the voice.   It rived his heart.

His stern determined look he took from off

The mortal place, and quick with fright he started

Back, recoil'd and dropt unstain'd upon the

    ground

His sheathless dirk, which high above her head ·

He held.

        Again he heard the voice upon

The midnight blast exclaim, "Outcast of earth

Is searching among these hills, to ravish

Helpless women, then to thrust them from you

As in scorn, to murder in cold blood

Thy vaunted chivalry ?   The crimes which you've

Already done, now cry aloud to Heaven

For vengeance.   Therefore, thou rebel reprobate!

Beware.   If you murder her nigh strangled

At your feet, hell's furies, that now thirst

Unceasing for your blood, will pursue you

Everywhere.   Horrid sounds will rise on

Ev'ry wind and in your blood-stained conscience

Howl these words : 'Seducer, coward, murderer.'"

Pale turned the chieftain's cheeks : His joints
    trembled

As if by an intermittent ague shook.

Then he quickly, like a fleeting shadow,

Vanish'd through the gloom, whilst the voice,
    meantime,

Hard on his trail, cried : " Thou curst, abandon'd
    wretch,

Well may'st thou fly from guilt's alarms,

But never from your wicked conscience.

CHAPTER X.

Daisy's Rescue—Her Deliverer—Her Meeting with
Athol—The Battle—Death of the Lovers.

WHEN the chieftain deep into the forest shade
Had fled, the stranger from his covert hied
To the gloomy spot where Daisy's cries for
Mercy had arisen, and found her there
Half dead by fear, murmuring in despair.

Soon he from the ground her faint form raised,
And in her livid cheeks beheld how much,
Alas! her inmost heart was wounded.   Then
From the rocky cell along a vernal path
He bore his fragile trust in safety,
Until a hazel glade he reached, where obscur'd
From curious sight, he halted near
A tinkling rill, which down a pebbly steep
Slow trickling ran, and with its ice-cool water
Daisy's fevered temples lav'd.

                                 Soon with
Open eyes she hailed the breaking morn's gray
    light ;
Her ears caught the plaintive murmur of the rill ;
Her low voice muttered, " Where am I ? By whom
Thus held hand bound ?   Who's my deliverer ?"

    'Twas then the stranger read with glad surprise
Her brighten'd looks, and thro' her gleaming eyes
Saw her life was safe ; but yet a symbol

There reveal'd some hidden secret in her heart,

Which, altho' her charms had been by the keen

    blight

Of sorrow faded, still show'd that the soft tinge

Of beauty lingered on her care-worn cheeks. .

"Oh, Sir," she said, "to you I owe my life,

To you my grateful thanks are due.   Never

Can my heart renounce thy hallow'd friendship's

    claim."

Then she told him all about her hard fate :

What wrongs she'd from the rebels borne, and how

Of father, mother, friends bereft ; and one,

Also, who found her young, torn from her fair.

"Ah !" she sigh'd, "oft together we have form'd

Our mutual faiths with fondest truths, and sealed,

With true love sighs, our promised hymen vow.

But being then of him and friends bereft

By that pamper'd son of vice and tyranny,

No one was left who could my griefs assuage ;

And oft I've visited the blissful bowers

Where we were wont to meet, and wander'd often

O'er and o'er again our fie᷄   of cheerful love ;

But all those once bright scenes were clouded ;

Nor sun, nor moon, nor stars had light for me.

Each hour his absence wrung my heart.   Many

Long, sad days I heard no tidings of him ;

And feared I was, alas! forever doom'd

His friendship's bitter loss to taste, when—" Here

She paused to wipe away the tears that dimm'd

Her eyes.

"Alas!" her friend then cried, "how strange

Do secret sympathies human souls pervade !

The hardest heart in grief like thine would feel

A share ; and even now to see thee weep,

Connects with thine my own remember'd joys

Unto thy wretchedness ; for thy plight afflicts

My heart, and, like me, I learn thou art to love

And keen despair a prey,—a victim of

The self same ruffian vile who thrust me in

A dungeon dark, where many weary days

14

And nights I, caged up like an untamed beast,

Imprison'd sat, a hapless vassal bound,

Pining in darkness, famish'd, and benumb'd

By damps, clanking my slavish chains, and
     counting

Many a weary hour of my dull life

Away, thinking that if I could but rend

The links that gall'd my heart, I'd quickly fly

To the dear pledge whom to my first-born hopes

Was known—one whose face I found in pride of

Beauty fair, and in whose lustrous blue eye

Her gentle spirit shone.   O that Daisy

Now were nigh to hear my voice, I'd—"

                                        Daisy felt

Like being lifted to the clouds, and fixed

Her eyes full on the stranger.   "I see, I see!"

She cried, "thou art none else but Athol!

This yeoman's guise is all delusion!"

With one accordant pause an attitude

They struck ; and mute awhile they stood in all

The silent eloquence of love ; then rush'd
Into each others' arms.

              Heart to heart they press'd—
Burning kisses seal'd their lips.   Raptures raised
Their two embodied souls to heaven, for
They knew not where they stood.   Creation, too,
Her grateful voice uplifted ; as the sky,
Just then, with joyous light an unclouded
Aspect wore.   Gaily the birds, in pairs,
On lithe wings flutter'd about them.   Their jocund
    songs
Attuned made the welkin ring with mirth.

Soon from the wretched Daisy Athol's presence
Banish'd care ; her falling tears dried, and caus'd
Life's mantling current high to mount her face.
Her humorous heart then dimpled her cheek with
Smiles.   The lucid gladness over all
Her features spread.   Sonorous and clear she
    vented

Forth a joyous laugh at seeing Athol

In disguise.   He, too, in sweet astonishment

Smiled and said : " 'Tis done to cheat the rebel's
    sight ;

For, the human mind, you know, is well versed

In deceit : The sire of falsehood practised

It ; the rebels follow him ; we copy

Them—perhaps with more consummate art."

                                        'Twas

Thus that their strange meeting on each other

Much unsullied pleasure did bestow.   Then

Daisy mildly said : " Come, Athol, let us

Hasten from this place : It is the shrine of

Rebels, and the air around is tainted

With their breaths.   Come, let us go ere the
    brood of

Vile cut-throats bar our paths."

                            " No, Daisy, no,"

Cried Athol, " Fame, honor, truth, forbid it.

The dastard sycophant who mock'd at me
Scarce heal'd of my wounds, and you an orphan
Made, to suffer from hunger and p'rhaps die,
Unpitied, among my friends a speedy fate
Must find : as justice for the wrongs the brute
Has done, the crimes which he's exulted o'er
Demand his doom.   Yet, being a scout, it would
Be prudent, now to leave ere danger may
In direst form arise and disconcert
My well laid plans to capture the guerrillas,
For our corps is now encamp'd upon the edge
Of this small stream just where it runs through
    yonder cedar grove."

    Then they clasped their hands and sighed the
    vow that
They would, when the battle ceased and he had
Swept with giant strength the proud survivor
Of their wrongs from earth, be wed.   So, Daisy,
Hailed the dawn of that bright day, thinking
    much

Of the sweet promise and of many years
Of bliss in store, and said whatever might
Betide, she'd share his fate on future fields
Of proud renown or fall with him in victory.
So, trusting in Heaven for strength and quick
With nimble feet she with him flew, to dare
The paths which Athol oft had dared before.

 Then ere the redd'ning sun that day had set,
Sounds of drums and war's alarms were heard
  upon
The wind. / Hosts of men with hollow eyes,
Haggard cheeks, and with their bright arms
  gleaming
In the sun, cross'd Potomac's flood to wage
Impious war upon Antietam's plain.   .
There McClellan brave, his country's pride, but
Short-lived faction's hate, unfurled his banner
To the vent'rous foe, and led in proud array
His daring thousands forth, who far and wide

Dispersed Lee's plund'ring hosts.

In Daisy's eyes
It was an awful sight to see, face to face,
Christian freemen stand in line of battle dread
Hurling ruin, waste, and death around her :
Terrible the vengeful shouts and horrid yells
Which rose amid the thundering cannon's peal :
Heart-rending cries of mortal agony,
And shrieks of death from mangled corse ascend-
    ing.

And when the discordant din of strife had
Died upon the evening breeze, she bounded
'Midst the heroic slain, and called, with cries
Of sadness, the name of him who promised
Her, ere long, the nuptial ring.   So, onward,
Wild in aspect, across the bloody plain
She flew, searching, with tearful eyes along,
With brothers o'er brothers bending, fathers
O'er slaughter'd sons, and friends loudly mingling

Their lamentations with the wounded's groans,

Her Athol's bleeding form ; when soon, among

The ghastly slain, she spied, prostrate upon

The ensanguined ground, the guerilla chief,

Athol's mortal foe, 'gainst whom he strove in

Rage of battle hot, and triumph'd o'er at last :

For, a deadly minie ball from Athol's

Well-aimed carbine had gone whizzing where

The chieftain stood, urging on his men, and sank
Him 'mid the rebel dead.

                 Seeing his fate,
She raised her hands on high, and utter'd "God
Be praised, thy retribution's just :" then hurried
On in grief, low bending, scrutinizing,
In the moon's pale beam, ev'ry pallid face
That lay cold in death, to find her love.

   Soon from the blood-stained grass a muttered
      prayer
With mournful groans upon her ears sounded.
Quickly whence the moans arose she hastened ;
And there, alas ! quite faint, expiring, saw
Her lover writhing in his wounds, bleeding
Fast, all welt'ring in his life blood, gasping
Hard for breath ; his dark hair drenched with
      gore ; his
Musket by his side, its handle firmly grasped.

Franticly, she called him by his name ; stooped
And fondly clasped her Athol to her heart,
Brushed the matted locks back from his brow and
Gazing on his dying eyes, she bade him speak

One dear fond word to her, his Daisy fair.

He muttered "Oh ! is that you, love, my bride ?"

Then gave a gurgling sound and lay a breathless
   corpse.

   Swift frenzy lit her eyes.   A mortal pang

Her heart struck.   She gave a shriek and cried
   aloud,

"Oh ! God, thy will be done," then fell upon

Her lover's clay-cold corse, kissed his bloodless lips

And on his mangled bosom died.

FINIS.